"Remember, I've got my eye on you."

"Maybe that's not what I want." She raised her chin at him, and he laughed, giving her a gentle pat on the bottom.

"Jackie, one thing I know about you is that you like me. You liked me well enough to have me on your sofa every Saturday night for the past five years. Nothing changed except you got pregnant, and now you have to somehow figure out how to get me to the altar."

He kissed her lips when they parted in outrage.

"It's okay," Pete said, "it may not be as hard as you think to get me there."

Dear Reader,

How excited I am to introduce you to the Callahans of Rancho Diablo in New Mexico! These six brothers are a bit wild, but they love their Aunt Fiona and Uncle Burke with all their hearts. When their mismanaging aunt is beset by a neighboring mischief maker determined to make a land grab for Rancho Diablo, all the brothers declare themselves willing to back her up. Fiona's answer, of course, is to try to marry off all her nephews as fast as she can and populate the ranch with babies. But there are many secrets at Rancho Diablo, and the brothers are going to have to decide who is on which side— something that isn't always easy when you have a cagey aunt and six men determined to outwit the altar!

I really enjoyed writing this series, and I hope you will enjoy reading about Pete, Creed, Judah, Rafe, Sam and Jonas. There's nothing I love more than telling tales about families and the ties that bind them together. It is my hope that you, too, hear the sound of the mythical wild Diablos as they paint the horizon at Rancho Diablo, and find magic in your own life!

All my best,

Tina

www.tinaleonard.com

@Tina_Leonard on Twitter

TinaLeonardBooks on Facebook

The Cowboy's Triplets
TINA LEONARD

TORONTO NEW YORK LONDON
AMSTERDAM PARIS SYDNEY HAMBURG
STOCKHOLM ATHENS TOKYO MILAN MADRID
PRAGUE WARSAW BUDAPEST AUCKLAND

Recycling programs
for this product may
not exist in your area.

ISBN-13: 978-0-373-75358-1

THE COWBOY'S TRIPLETS

Copyright © 2011 by Tina Leonard

This edition published by arrangement with Harlequin Books S.A.

For questions and comments about the quality of this book please contact us at Customer_eCare@Harlequin.ca.

www.Harlequin.com

Printed in U.S.A.

ABOUT THE AUTHOR

Tina Leonard is a bestselling author of more than forty projects, including a popular thirteen-book miniseries for Harlequin American Romance. Her books have made the Waldenbooks, Ingram and Nielsen BookScan bestseller lists. Tina feels she has been blessed with a fertile imagination and quick typing skills, excellent editors and a family who loves her career. Born on a military base, she lived in many states before eventually marrying the boy who did her crayon printing for her in the first grade. Tina believes happy endings are a wonderful part of a good life. You can visit her at www.tinaleonard.com.

Books by Tina Leonard

Many thanks go to Kathleen Scheibling,
for believing in this series and always
having faith in me, and editing my work
with a sure hand. There are many people at
Harlequin who make my books ready for
publication, most of whom I will never have the
chance to thank in person, and they have my
heartfelt gratitude. Also many thanks to
my children and my husband,
who are enthusiastic and supportive,
and most of all, the generous readers who are
the reason for my success.

Chapter One

"A dark night for Peter D. Callahan is being alone in his room."

—Jeremiah Callahan,
who knew his toddler son all too well.

"The Diablos are running." Pete Callahan turned from the frost-speckled window, letting his words sink into the sudden silence. His five brothers and Aunt Fiona looked at him.

A shiver touched Pete. The shadowy, misty mustangs running like the wind across the far reaches of the ranch meant magic was in the cold night air. According to legend, the Diablos only ran as a portent of something mystical to come. The Diablos were real—and magical in themselves—but Pete didn't believe in mystical magic, the oogie-boogie kind of magic. Nor did he believe in pushy old beloved aunts trying to rule from the grave, as his aunt Fiona was hinting she would.

Jonas Callahan ignored his brother's inopportune comment and resumed gently badgering their dear aunt. "You've suggested your time is running out," Jonas said to Fiona, who shrugged, dismissing the light sarcasm in his tone. Fiona was holding court in the massive library at Rancho Diablo in New Mexico. His brothers lounged around the room in various states of stubbled beards and dirty jeans, fresh from working the ranch. They were trying to assuage her worries, let her know that they were there for her in all matters—though if anybody did not need help, it was their cagey aunt.

"I am seventy-nine," Fiona said. "Please speak to me with respect. You make me sound as reliable as a vintage bedside clock."

"You've just told us that you're leaving Rancho Diablo to one of us based on a dream you had," Pete said. "We're more interested in your health than in your will, Aunt Fiona."

"Oh, poppycock." She sniffed, clearly put out with her six nephews. No doubt she thought they were trying to mollify her, coddle her to get into her good graces. It annoyed Pete.

"You all want Rancho Diablo because it was your parents'," Fiona said. "Let's be honest about our motivations."

If that wasn't calling the kettle black.

"Aunt Fiona, I speak for all of us—" Pete gestured toward his sprawling brothers who were only too content to allow him to beard their celestial-minded, determined aunt "—when I say that we don't believe in dreamscapes, incantations, voodoo or rubbing the venerated bellies of mystical bunnies dating from the time of Lewis Carroll. So our motivation is simple. We love you. Most of us live here at Rancho Diablo because we love you, as much as you seem inclined to look for an ulterior motive. The ranch is our livelihood, but it isn't everything."

Murmurs of assent rose from his brothers. His aunt gave him a disapproving, sour look. She was a tiny woman, a petite bundle of dynamite in a prim navy-blue wool dress. Her only concession to the bitter cold was what she called her bird boots—knee-high, lugged soles, fur-lined. White hair was pulled severely back from her face in an elegant updo she called a bird's nest. It did have the same sort of peculiar order of a mourning dove's nest, but it was attractive. There wasn't a spare ounce of flesh on the diminutive woman, which made people at first meeting assume she was fragile.

She was not.

"Nevertheless," Fiona said, her eyes bright behind her glasses, "I am following my dream."

"You do that." Pete crouched to stoke the fire. He wondered if it would be easier on their beloved aunt if he had gas-lit logs installed in the seven fireplaces throughout the huge ranch house, and decided she'd resent the implication that she couldn't take care of her home herself. The smell of cookies hung in the air, lingering with the fragrances of Christmas and home, which was, Pete thought, how their wily aunt managed to lure her nephews to the house so often, although they would have surreptitiously checked on her and Burke anyway. Home-baked cookies and other to-die-for gastronomic delights—they simply had it too good, courtesy of Fiona.

"Since Pete doesn't care about his stake in Rancho Diablo, that leaves it to the rest of you to see which of you will take over the ranch. When I'm gone, naturally. Which might be any day now." She held a tissue to her nose. "This is the third cold I've had this month. My immune system is so weak."

Jonas straightened. "You said nothing about feeling weak."

"Not that you would care, Doctor." She rubbed her glasses clean and replaced them on her pert nose. "Burke, please bring the brandy. We are all in need of a bit of fortification. Except Pete, who is always above the fray."

Her faithful butler went to do her bidding. Pete sighed and sat down on the leather sofa, where he had a premier seat to stare out the window at the frozen landscape. Guilt was a familiar parenting tool, and she'd been employing it with greater frequency of late. The problem was, he knew all about Fiona's Secret Plan, so he had plenty of guilt heaping on him from all sides. It sucked being the responsible one. "I'll take the damn brandy," he said as Burke offered him a snifter. Right now, he could use a stiff one.

"The terms of the deal—which have also been written into my revised will—are thus. The first of you who gets married to a suitable woman, has a family and settles down, will inherit Rancho Diablo. You may not sell the land or house, of course, without all six of you being in agreement. That is what was revealed to me in my dream."

Pete sighed. Their stubborn aunt was hatching more mayhem for their lives. He knew she was serious about this plan, and the mischievous side of him thought she was cute and downright smart to try to pull this on his brothers, who richly deserved the trap Fiona was springing on them. They'd fall for it, too, in his opinion, though they should know better. Nobody left ranches worth millions of dollars in land value alone to relatives based on a dream, not to mention expecting them to compete for it, especially not using the tool of marriage. None of them even had a serious girlfriend. Pete scowled at his brothers.

The problem was that the plan was sound—but the material Fiona had to work with was sadly lacking.

There was Jonas, the eldest, a successful surgeon who

surely had his pick of hot doctors and nurses. He kept himself busy amassing a reputation as a hard-working, best-in-class cardiac guy. Jonas was a typical girl-magnet: tall, dark as the ace of spades, square-jawed. All good stuff, but clueless with women, basically a bonehead with every subject except science and research. A typical nerd, and useless to Fiona's Secret Plan, in Pete's opinion.

Pete continued the roll call. There was Creed, who wouldn't send women screaming from his appearance, but was too wild for most men, let alone women. Creed was a typical badass, the kind of man ladies loved like grandmas loved tea. Creed, unfortunately, would never love anything but rodeo and the ranch. No marriage material there.

Creed's twin, Rafe, was a strange blend of nerd and reckless cowboy. Sometimes he wore his long jet-black hair in a braid down his back. Other times he shaved his head. The best way Pete could describe his free-spirited brother was "out there"—egregiously, studiously out there on the edge. One day a woman might reel him back in to planet Earth, but Pete wouldn't put down a twenty on it.

Judah was a champion bullrider. He had ladies in every town. He was popular with everyone, and blessed with good fortune and athleticism. Judah's face was cut by the hand of Michelangelo: strong, precise and manly. Women left undies in his gear with phone numbers. One enterprising young lady had herself carried into his hotel room in a maid's cart. Judah hadn't been able to resist the French maid's costume, nor the heiress who'd wanted a cowboy fling and had flown him to Paris for a weekend of French cuisine and French-kissing and everything else that entailed. Judah was a kind, damaged soul and ladies adored all that haunted mystique. But Judah had never chosen just one woman to be his girl. Pete thought Judah overworked the Eeyore routine, but he had to admit it worked brilliantly for his brother.

Finally, there was Sam. No one needed to worry about Sam's zeal for the altar. Stockier and more muscular than the rest of them (which meant he could kick just about anybody's ass who messed with him), Sam carried a chip on his shoulder that had everything to do with confidence, swagger and being the youngest. He knew there was something different about him, which didn't help. He'd come "later" as Jonas always put it, and Pete thought Sam had grown up not exactly understanding his place in the world or the family. Nobody worked harder than Sam, but then sometimes Sam would disappear for days.

Pete shook his head. Fiona was barking up all kinds of wrong trees with this latest plan. He'd consider his brothers candidates for group therapy rather than matrimonial bliss. *But that's just me,* he thought, *and I tend to be a doubter.*

He supposed he'd be the closest to suiting Fiona's ridiculous offer. He at least had a Saturday-night thing going on. Still, being Mr. Saturday Night wasn't likely to be upped to two nights a week, much less a full lifetime.

Pete sighed. He admired their Irish aunt who loved to dabble in drama. He had to hand it to her—there was never a moment when she wasn't trying to fix their lives. Fiona certainly had her work cut out for her this time, but he knew she would stick to it until she considered her job done and done well.

"When was this dream?" Jonas asked, shifting his long legs as he reached for another Christmas cookie from the silver platter on the side table. Pete thought a heart surgeon should be watching his cholesterol, or at least the toxic-waste levels in his body, but no one could eat just one of Fiona's cookies. Jonas could be counted on to talk some sense into the redoubtable aunt, and Pete relaxed a little. Surely the rest of the brothers could see that there were as many holes in this plan as in Swiss cheese—and his guilt would go away once he knew they'd safely figured Fiona out. After all, what would stop any of them—all of them—from running out, hiring a woman to fake a marriage and perhaps a pregnancy, and then cashing in? Pete swallowed, not wanting to think about his little aunt pushing up daisies.

"It wasn't so much a dream, it was more a *premonition*," Fiona said. "It occurred when I talked to a nice lady at the traveling carnival."

Creed sat up. "Traveling carnival?"

"That's right. She was standing outside her tent. There was a sign on it that read Madame Vivant's Fortune-Telling. Several of the ladies from the Books 'n' Bingo Society decided it sounded like fun. So we went in."

Pete heard Rafe groan. He agreed with the sentiment. Was their adorable, feisty aunt beginning to show the start of some affliction that would affect her mental capacity? His blood ran cold at the thought.

"As a matter of fact, I've invited her here tonight. Burke, please show Madame Vivant into the library."

Pete watched as his lunkheaded brothers seemed to transmogrify in the face of a beautiful woman. Jonas looked like a petrified tree felled by an ax, and the rest of his brothers were practically drooling like babies. He was embarrassed for them. Pete smelled enticing perfume, heard the jingle of tiny charms she wore on silver bracelets. No more than five foot two, Madame

Vivant was a delightful babe of about twenty-five. He'd bet the whole "dream" was a ruse for her to get hitched to one of them. Madame Fortune-teller his ass—more like Madame Shakedown Artist.

This was bad news. No woman of good intent should jingle when she walked. It was as *look-at-me!* as a lady could get.

Pete decided Fiona's scheme was getting out of hand. She wasn't supposed to bring the catnip to the mice, was she? It was dirty pool, and he had to draw the line somewhere.

A guy could only enjoy watching his brothers get worked over by Fiona for so long.

"You have to leave," Pete said, towering over the tiny redhead. He refused to notice the trim waist, the delightful peachy bosom, the sweetly curved hips under the undulating black skirt that had his easily-led-astray brothers reeling. Once again, Pete realized, it was up to him to save them from themselves. "Take your bells and your parlor tricks out of here. And don't bother taking Burke's pocket watch," he said, neatly removing it from the velvet pouch she carried. He'd seen it poking out and recognized it instantly. It was one of the butler's prized possessions.

Burke cleared his throat. "I gave her that, sir. I asked her to help me with a personal matter."

Pete looked at the butler he'd known ever since Burke and Fiona had come to the ranch to care for the boys. He softened his words for Burke—he'd protect him, too. "No doubt she has played with your mind as well. Never mind. Once you're off the property, Madame Vivant—if that is your real name—all will be right again."

Cool green eyes considered him. "Tough guy, huh?"

"That's right. Off you go, little gypsy." Pete congratulated himself on his excellent handling of the situation—until Jonas spoke up.

"Not so fast, bro," Jonas said. "It's cold outside. I'm sure we could offer our guest a cup of cocoa, couldn't we, Burke?"

The butler nodded and went off to do Jonas's bidding. Jonas continued staring at the gypsy as if his brain was locked in gear. Pete scowled. Surely Jonas—steady-handed Jonas the surgeon—wouldn't get the hots for a *gypsy*.

He should have put a stop to this in the beginning; he was practically an accomplice. But he hadn't counted on his brothers being super boneheads—just greedy. He opened his mouth to throw water on the scheme, confess everything, too, but Fiona shot him down.

"Pete!" His aunt's voice cracked like a whip. "You're being rude to an invited guest, and one thing we aren't at Rancho Diablo is *rude*."

He shrugged and went to lean against a wall. "If you think I'm going to be part of a séance or machination on her part to confuse you, I'm afraid we're not going to fall for the plan, Aunt." There, that was a piece of delicious Broadway acting, if he did say so himself—although he was still worried about Jonas. Sam was young and hotheaded, so he might have expected Sam to latch on to their visitor, or wild-at-heart Creed might have been an easy target. Any of them but Jonas, who was still stonelike and staring—rapt, mesmerized.

Creed, Rafe, Judah and Sam all crossed their arms, gazing with interest at the fortune-teller. They seemed very interested in the tale she was about to spin. Pete would have to keep a close eye on Fiona since no one else seemed inclined to play protector to their giddy aunt.

The next thing Pete knew, Jonas was lying on the

floor staring up at the wood-beamed ceiling. Madame Vivant stood over him, staring down at his brother. Jonas said, "My lucky, lucky eyes," and Pete wondered if Jonas had hit his head on the way down. Pete was getting really nervous. He glanced at Fiona to see if she was worried about the effects of her Secret Plan, but she seemed more interested in the warm drink Burke was handing her.

"What happened?" Jonas asked as Madame Vivant moved to help him up.

"You fainted," she told him.

Jonas raised a disbelieving brow that made Pete proud. For a moment he'd feared his older brother was going to drown in a pool of misplaced desire.

"I'm a doctor, and a damn good one. I think I'd know if I'd fainted."

"You fainted, bro," Rafe said. "Went down like a sack of hammers."

"Made a real funky sound when you fell, too," Aunt Fiona said. "When you were just a little thing, I used to ask you if you'd stepped on a frog when you made that noise, Jonas. Brings back memories—"

"That's enough." Jonas stared at the petite redhead. "You did something to me."

"You don't believe in spells," she replied. "A doctor wouldn't believe in such things, would you?" She took his hand in her much smaller one and helped him to his feet with a surprisingly strong yank.

"I felt fine before you walked in," Jonas replied, his voice crabby, and Pete relaxed. Jonas had obviously recovered his good sense when he fell out of his chair, or whatever the hell he'd just done. *We're all working too hard. Or we've had too much Christmas vacation with the holiday-loving aunt.*

"Can we get on with this?" Aunt Fiona asked, her

tone impatient. "Madame Vivant can't stay long. The carnival's train moves on tonight."

"After she's stolen the family heirlooms," Pete muttered.

"We don't have any of those," Sam said. "Bro, sit over here so I can keep an eye on you. You're making an ass of yourself."

This was tough coming from the baby. He'd changed that boy's diapers! Pete felt tired suddenly, and not soothed by the brandy Burke pressed on him.

"Your aunt asked me here to interpret—explain—the dream she had while in my tent," Madame Vivant said. "Your family home is in jeopardy."

Pete rolled his eyes. He couldn't help it. He knew he was being churlish, and a thirty-one-year-old man shouldn't be. Of course the family home was in danger. The culprit was sitting next to his aunt on her velvet footstool. Why couldn't anyone but him see this?

His brothers were mesmerized. They leaned forward like schoolboys, hanging on every word that dropped from Madame Vivant's sweet ruby lips. Even Jonas went back to being spellbound, looking as if he might jump into her lap any second. Pete just glared at her. "In danger from what?" he demanded. "Or whom?"

As if he didn't know.

"That has not been revealed to me," the fortune-teller replied, her voice soft.

He shook his head. "And so we're all supposed to get married, and have a child—"

"That's your aunt's solution," the gypsy said.

"Look," Pete said, tired of the conversation. He and his brothers had work to do on the ranch. He didn't want to leave this woman here to prey on his innocent aunt's fears. She loved Rancho Diablo with all her heart. She'd kept it running after their mother and father had died, had raised all of them to manhood. He was always up for a joke on his hammerheaded brothers, but Aunt Fiona's scheme was getting out of hand.

Suddenly, Jonas spoke. "I'm not going to allow you to continue this charade until you tell me your real name. This Madame Vivant crap is for beginners, and I am no easy mark. I want your name in case I have to have the law hunt you down."

Her eyes widened.

"Jonas!" Fiona leaned forward. "I'm going to ask you to leave if you insist upon being a pest."

Jonas refused to release the gypsy's gaze. Something was definitely happening to his normally uptight brother.

"My name," she finally said, "is Sabrina McKinley."

"Your real name? Or one of many aliases? I've got a good mind to call the cops right now," Jonas stated, and Pete was pretty certain his brother meant it. Jonas seemed to be fluctuating between protecting their aunt and rampant sexual desire, and if he wasn't so worried, Pete might have enjoyed the drama.

"It's my real name." She stared back at Jonas, unafraid of his growing ire. "I might remind you that I don't know any of you. I came alone, knowing there would be six men and only a frail elderly woman here—"

Pete expected his aunt to utter a loud "ha!" but she only sighed and pulled an afghan around her shoulders.

"You've convinced her she's ill," Jonas said, outraged. "She was fine last I saw her. You've toyed with her mind, made her think she's dying—"

Madame Vivant—Sabrina—shook her head. "I have no dark powers."

"Hypnotism isn't a dark art?"

She gasped. "How dare you?"

"Let her finish, Jonas," Rafe said, interrupting the two verbal combatants. "She's not going to hurt anybody by saying whatever she wants to say."

"I'm going to do this," Fiona said, "in fact, I've already changed my will. Regardless of what misguided thoughts you have about my mental state, the time has come for me to make a decision about Rancho Diablo." She looked around at all of her nephews. "Which of you truly feels a special connection to Rancho Diablo? Would want it to be yours? You, Jonas, are the eldest," Fiona said, "and marriage might suit you."

"And you have a bid on a ranch sixty miles to the east," Sabrina said. "You've been thinking about having your *own* working ranch."

Pete supposed she expected them to be amazed that she knew this bit of information, as if they were in the presence of a mystical mind-reader. Pete *was* surprised his brother was thinking about owning a ranch in New Mexico, since he had a successful surgical practice in Dallas, Texas. Fiona must have told Sabrina.

"Sorry, I don't feel like cooperating," Jonas said, sounding more in control of his faculties, to Pete's relief. "I'm not getting married, having a baby or playing hoodwink-the-gentle-aunt."

"Nevertheless, you will be considered, Jonas," Fiona said, her tone firm. "Should you marry and produce multiple heirs, you will be considered for Rancho Diablo."

"Multiple heirs?" Creed asked.

"Naturally," Fiona said. "Whichever of you has the *largest* family should inherit the property, which makes sense on several levels. That's what Madame Vivant suggested, and I think it's an excellent plan to ensure that none of you try to hire a woman with a child to fool me or my executor." She shot Jonas a stern look. "It's not like my own kin doesn't know a little something about hoodwinking the gentle aunt."

Pete silently conceded Fiona's point. Over the years they had done their best to pull the wool over the bright aunty eyes, with varying degrees of success. She'd grown up on a farm in Ireland with eleven brothers, so she knew a lot about what boys—men—could get into. It had been like living with a kindly old jailer.

Still, they'd done their best—and had occasionally succeeded.

"Now, I don't expect any of this to happen overnight," Aunt Fiona continued. "In fact, given the nature of your extreme bachelorhoods, it could be *years* before any of you settle down. Therefore, I have set forth these plans with an executor in an airtight will and testament. *Airtight.*"

Pete rose to his feet. "Jonas, you get the job of trying to talk sense into our beloved aunt."

Jonas smiled a lazy come-and-get-it smile at the gypsy. "I'm not so certain Aunt Fiona's plan doesn't have some merit. I'm not totally opposed to settling down."

Pete had expected all five of his brothers to follow him out the door in a cavalcade of loyalty and righteous indignation. But to a man, they wouldn't look at him.

He was outnumbered, voted down. Aunt Fiona's Secret Plan was surely succeeding beyond her wildest dreams.

"Fine. I'm going to check on the horses. Then I'm bedding down. None of you, and that includes you, Jonas," he said, sweeping a hand toward his brothers, "come crying to me when you find yourselves ensnared by Mata Hari here."

By that moniker he meant their aunt as well—she was

such a bad storyteller—but Sabrina looked at Jonas with big, sexy, fake-concerned eyes. *Oh, boy,* Pete thought. *That's danger dressed in a sweet tight top all right. Jonas is a marked man.*

He decided it would be fun to watch Jonas fall like a granite boulder for a woman. Pete grinned, suddenly feeling no guilt at all.

Jonas stood, catching Pete by surprise. "Well, I'm out like a trout," Jonas said. "It was a pleasure meeting you," he told Madame Vivant.

"You can't leave," Pete said, "The fun's just beginning."

"I've got patients," Jonas reminded him. "Got to catch a plane back to Dallas. Pete, I leave tonight's discussion and everything that follows in your more-than-capable hands."

"Oh, hell, no," Pete said. "Don't you leave me holding the bag, Jonas."

"Sorry. Duty calls."

"Duty?" Pete realized Jonas was really leaving. This was bad for Fiona's trap. Pete didn't want her trap slamming shut on *him.* "Jonas, we have a problem here."

"No worries," Jonas said, kissing their aunt goodbye. "You'll take care of everything, Pete." He departed as though he hadn't spent the past half hour ogling the gypsy like a tomcat eyeing a nice, juicy mouse.

Pete glanced at his aunt, wondering if Jonas's exit blew up her plan, but she was staring at him as though she expected him to do something, and Pete sighed.

It was hell being Mr. Responsibility.

Chapter Two

Pete hadn't exactly meant to tell Jonas to blow it out his ass, but when his older brother pulled a fast escape, leaving him in charge of a room full of lunatics, Pete wondered if he'd yanked Jonas's chain a bit hard. He hadn't seen his brother's gaze light on a woman like it had lit on Madame Vivant in…well, since Nancy had left him at the altar five years ago.

Madame Vivant—Sabrina McKinley—wasn't a woman who had accosted their tender aunt with a wild story to prey on her feebleness. Pete had taken Fiona and her blue-rinsed friends to the fair. He'd happened to be standing outside the tent when Fiona and her three co-conspirators had hatched the plan with Sabrina. Hatched and hired, while he'd listened through the walls of the tent. He'd tried hard not to laugh. It wasn't such a bad plan. And he would never give away Fiona's Secret. His brothers had this one coming to them. If there had ever been a group of guys who needed to be thinking about their futures a bit more, it was probably the Callahan brothers.

Himself excluded, of course. He could just sit back and watch the fun as his brothers scrambled to win the ranch.

He eyed the door through which Jonas had departed.

Their more surly, tightly controlled brother wouldn't be able to stand the suspense. He'd be back, unable to keep himself from interfering. Jonas loved Fiona. The doctor in him wouldn't be able to stand the thought that he hadn't given her a decent evaluation. He'd think *strong pulse, lungs clear, heart rate excellent,* but all the while Jonas would be worrying like crazy. That was part of Fiona's MO, tugging on just the right heartstrings.

Pete leaned back, winked at Madame Vivant, and grinned. This would be great entertainment during January, a traditionally long, cold month on the ranch.

"Get your popcorn," he told Sabrina.

"I beg your pardon?" She glanced back at the door through which Jonas had exited.

Pete smiled. "He's a bit of a hothead."

She raised her chin and turned to Fiona. "I must be going, Miss Callahan."

Four brothers jumped up to walk her to the door. "Stay," Sabrina said. "I don't need to be walked to my car."

"Goodbye!" Fiona got up and made her way to the door, gently pushing her nephews out of her way. "Thank you so much for coming out. Good luck at your next stops! *Adh mór ort!*"

Sabrina went out with a jingle of bells and reluctant sighs from his brothers.

"You shouldn't listen to people like that, Aunt Fiona," Creed said. "Cute as she is, that fortune-teller doesn't know any more than the weatherman about what lies in the weeks ahead."

"That's right," Judah said. "We're going to take good care of you."

"Always," Rafe said.

And Sam said, "You better believe it."

Fiona blinked. "I don't want you boys looking after me. I want you looking for wives!"

Pete chuckled, deciding to give Fiona's plan a boost. "Wouldn't hurt to have some pretty ladies around this place."

Creed glared at him with indignation. "Women cause nothing but trouble."

"That's true," Judah said. "Did you ever see a more miserable man than Jonas when Nancy ran off?"

Rafe shook his head. "It would take more than a woman to get me to the altar. I love this ranch, Aunt Fiona, but damn, I'm not putting my neck in a noose to get it."

Sam shrugged. "I'm afraid I agree with them, Aunt. A woman just isn't worth all the heartache."

Fiona's jaw dropped. Pete almost felt sorry for her.

"Do you mean you intend *never* to marry? None of you?" she demanded.

Four brothers shook their heads.

"I've got plenty to do around here," Creed said. "No woman wants to be abandoned for the life of a cowboy."

"They all want to play *Desperate Housewives* these days," Rafe said. "High maintenance is not for me."

"But surely there are women out there, women from this very town, who are of stock that can appreciate this way of life?" Fiona said.

"Aunt," Judah said, his voice gentle, "we live two hundred miles from the nearest city. We live on five thousand acres of dirt. There are no malls, no restaurants—"

"There's Banger's Bait and Tackle," Fiona said. "They serve a mean catfish. Not to mention Mr. Sooner has been grilling burgers in his backyard for the last twenty-five years, and they're the best I've ever put in my mouth. You can't get a finer burger!"

Sam rearranged the wool afghan around his aunt's shoulders. "Don't worry," he said, kissing her cheek. "You and Burke can live here as long as you want. We'll work the ranch, the way we always have. We just don't want you getting so upset."

Fiona blinked, then looked at Pete. "You're awfully quiet, nephew."

He didn't know what to say. Truth was, he'd had his eye on a gal for quite some time, in fact, for the past fifteen or so years. But Jackie Samuels was less inclined to settle down than he was. She'd said a hundred times that what was between them—*their big secret*—was all she wanted. He couldn't figure that out. Wasn't a girl supposed to want to drag a man to the altar? Wasn't that part of the fun? She did the chasing, and he did the complaining, while she enticed him to the state of wedded bliss?

When Pete had asked her that, Jackie had shot back, "Why should I buy the steer when I can get the steak for free?" It was a question he hadn't considered before.

Pete went to stare out the window. Darkness had fallen so that all was visible was a wide range of inky nothing. They needed to put spotlights up in the trees around the ranch, and maybe some lamps on the fences. That reminded him—Jackie had a window or two at her tiny cottage he'd noticed needed repairing as well.

"I'm going out for a while," Pete announced. He felt sorry for Fiona because her Secret Plan had blown up on her, after she'd gone to the trouble of hiring an actress to help spin her diabolical and amusing web. Pete felt more sorry for himself, though, because he didn't stand a chance with the woman he loved.

Jackie Samuels had nursed enough grumpy patients in her life to develop a fairly thick skin, but Mr. Dearborn was about to make a dent in her good temper.

"I don't want to take any medicine," Mr. Dearborn said.

Jackie said, "Doctor's orders, Mr. Dearborn. You need to take this antibiotic, and then I'm going to give you a pneumonia shot. It's important to keep you well this winter so you don't have to come back." She handed him a glass of water.

Recognizing the take-no-prisoners tone of her voice, Mr. Dearborn took the medicine, then bared an arm for the injection.

"All done. Didn't hurt a bit, did it?"

"No," Mr. Dearborn said, "but I'd rather you quit bothering me."

"And you'd rather not be in this hospital." She covered him with a warm blanket and gave him a smile. "Try to get some rest before I bring you a small treat."

His face lit up. "Chocolate?"

"Yes." She placed a hand on his wrist, taking a pulse while he was thinking about his treat. "But you have to stop complaining every time I bring you your medicine. Please."

He wrinkled his nose, his white brows beetling. "You realize that when I complain, you bring me chocolate."

She sighed and took her clipboard from the table. "Yes, I do, Mr. Dearborn. I'll be back later."

She left his room and returned to the nurses' station. "Why do men have to play games?" she asked Darla Cameron.

"It's in their DNA," Darla answered. She looked at Jackie, her bright-blue gaze excited. "You're never going to believe it, but Candy Diamond has decided to sell her wedding-gown business."

Jackie blinked. "Isn't that bad? Diamond's Bridal is the only place to shop for gowns and nice dresses for two hundred miles."

"It might be bad," Darla said, "except you and I are going to buy the business."

Jackie shook her head. "I want no part of wedding gowns and nervous brides. I get enough complaining around here as it is."

Darla flopped some papers down in front of her. "And yet, check out the income from Candy's business."

Jackie stared at Darla for a moment, realizing her friend was serious. Her gaze moved to the column of figures and the paperwork Darla was tapping with a graceful finger. "Why is she selling if her business is so lucrative?"

"Needs to retire. And so do we," Darla told her. "Think of it, Jackie. No more bossy doctors. No more grumpy patients. We'd be our own bosses."

Jackie thought about Mr. Dearborn, one of her favorite patients. She liked caring for people. Sometimes the hours were long, but she was single. There was no one to inconvenience in her life. No family counting on her.

No husband, either. Pete Callahan, the secret love of her life, didn't care when she worked. Pete was the only man she'd ever made love with. He would marry her in a flash, he always told her—not that she believed him. He was an inveterate footloose cowboy, an enigmatic Prince Charming who claimed he was in it for the real kiss, only to drift off at the last second.

This bridal shop might be the closest she ever got to

being a bride. "I don't know," Jackie said. "What do we know about running a business?"

"My mom runs the Books 'n' Bingo," Darla said. "I've learned a bit about managing a mom-and-pop shop."

"But brides," Jackie said, thinking about all the drama involved with weddings, "there's a reason they're called bridezillas."

Darla shrugged. "It'd be nice to do something new for a change. I wouldn't mind smelling gardenias and lilies instead of antiseptic and other things. Not that I don't love most of my patients," Darla said, "but I'm ready for a new challenge."

"I guess you're right." Jackie looked at the line of figures again, her heart beginning to race with some excitement and a little trepidation. "Let me think about it tonight, okay? I need to come up with all the reasons I can why this is a very bad idea."

"I'd let your name be first on the door," Darla said.

Jackie blinked. "Samuels and Cameron's Bridal Shop? I think we'd be better off with something else."

Darla smiled. "Or Callahan," she suggested. "Callahan and Cameron."

"No." Jackie grabbed a wrapped piece of chocolate from her purse to take to Mr. Dearborn. "Even if I go into the wedding-gown business with you, Darla, I guarantee none of those gowns will ever be on my body." She only loved Pete, and the fact was, Pete only loved Rancho Diablo. He teased her about marriage, but both of them knew that he wasn't serious. Underneath it all, Pete was happy with their noncommitted-committed relationship. They kept quiet about it, they met in absolute secrecy, keeping the town busybodies from planning their wedding and naming their future children—and after all these years, she couldn't change the game. She had nothing to offer him in the way of family, if he wanted that, and surely he did.

They'd never talked about it. But even Pete had to notice, with his penchant for making love "bareback" as he put it, that a pregnancy had never arisen. There'd never even been a false alarm. It wasn't that she was taking unnecessary chances; she was over thirty. She would have been thrilled to become pregnant. Even just making love on Saturday nights should have produced a bingo at some point.

She was infertile.

"Maybe once Pete sees you around all those beautiful white gowns, he'll pop the question," Darla said.

"I don't think I can get pregnant," Jackie said, "and I'm pretty sure he would want a big family like his own."

Darla stared at her. "Aren't you on the pill?" she asked in a whisper.

Jackie shook her head. "I rarely have a cycle. In all my life, I've probably had ten."

Darla thought about that for a minute. "Maybe Pete's been fixed. Or maybe he has a problem."

Jackie laughed. "He has problems, but I don't think fathering a baby would be one."

"Some men have low sperm counts."

"Maybe." Pete was pretty virile, though. Jackie wouldn't bank on him having a problem.

"Well, anyway. Think about the bridal shop. We'll worry about getting Pete Callahan to the altar later. I'm sure we can spring a proper trap if we put our heads together." Darla went off, whistling, to check her patients.

"That's not what I meant!" Jackie called after her. Darla waved a backward hand at her and kept going.

But it was true. Jackie wasn't ever going to marry Pete. She knew it just as certainly as she knew the stars were going to shine in the dark New Mexico skies tonight. If she could get pregnant—maybe. But a family man would want a family, and so far, she wasn't a baby-mama kind of girl.

I'd love Pete's babies.

Short of magic, it wasn't likely.

"DON'T WORRY SO MUCH," Pete said as he climbed back through the bedroom window of Jackie's small house. "If you're going to jump around like that, I'm going to nail my finger. Then you'll have to nurse me."

Since there was nothing sexier than Jackie in her nurse's uniform, he really wouldn't mind her taking very good care of him. But she didn't laugh, the way she usually did. She watched him fit the frame a second more, then she left the room. He made sure it slid shut without a whisper, then followed her into the kitchen.

"Coffee?" she asked, avoiding his hands when he reached to grab her.

"Just you," he said, "as usual."

"Pete," Jackie said, "I think I'll go to bed early."

He looked at her, admiring her dark hair, darker eyes. She had springy little buns and an energy he loved, and he couldn't wait to get her in the sack. Why else did a man fix a woman's windows when they warped from drifting snow? He couldn't wait to run his hands over that perky butt. She had a back that curved just right into his body, and a—

"Pete, I don't know how to tell you this," Jackie said, and he tried to snap his focus back to where it needed to be. His little turtledove was awfully jumpy. Tonight was clearly going to be conversation-first night, and he was okay with that. As long as he got to hold her, Jackie could talk all she liked. "Go ahead. I'm listening."

"All right." Jackie turned delicious dark eyes the color of pure dark cocoa on him. He watched her lips as she hesitated. God, he loved her mouth. If she wanted to talk for an hour, he'd just sit and watch with pleasure. As long as she let him kiss that mouth, he was a happy man.

"I think it's time for us to…"

He grinned. "To what, sugar?" He had a feeling he knew where this was going, and it couldn't be more timely.

"I'm so sorry, Pete," Jackie said, taking a deep breath. "But I don't want to see you anymore."

Chapter Three

The jackass—he actually *laughed*. Jackie stared at Pete, all the tears she'd been trying not to cry drying up to nothing.

"Come here," he said, reaching for her, "you're tired. You've had a bad day. Come tell big ol' Pete all about it."

She squirmed out of his arms, though she never had before. "No. It's nothing like that. It's just time, Pete."

He watched her, his dark-blue eyes wide with unspoken questions. Pete wasn't the kind of man who talked a lot. He wouldn't bug her to death about what she was thinking. In a minute, he'd shrug, decide the pastures were greener elsewhere, and off he'd go.

She just had to wait out this awkward moment.

Yet, as his gaze refused to release hers, she knew she'd not only caught him by complete surprise, somehow she'd also wounded him. She was shocked by that more than anything.

"Jackie, you mean a bunch to me," Pete said.

"And you mean a lot to me." Jackie reexamined her feelings for the hundredth time, and came to the same conclusion as before: It was time to end what was a nonserious relationship between them. Maybe these new feelings had started when Mr. Dearborn protested his medicine—for the hundredth time. Perhaps it had been knowing that nothing was going to change about her life, not tomorrow or the next day, if she didn't stop going along with the currents that flowed in their predictable patterns in Diablo.

But when Darla had mentioned changing their entire livelihoods, Jackie had known she was being handed the only chance she might ever have to change her whole life.

Maybe it shouldn't have meant ending her relationship with Pete, too, but what she had with him was just as much of a road to nowhere as anything else. By the hurt expression on his face, she wondered if she was being selfish. But the bottom line was that she was in love with Pete Callahan, and he was not in love with her, and after fifteen years of loving the man and five years of sleeping with him, she knew their pattern was just as predictable as any other in her week. She would find him in her bed, he would ravish her, adore her body from toe to nose and then he'd depart before dawn to feed cattle and horses.

And she'd see him again—the next Saturday.

"I'm sorry," she said to the pain she saw in his eyes.

And he said, "I am, too, sugar." He stroked one work-roughened hand down her chin-length hair, then her cheek, put his hat on and left.

This should feel different, Jackie thought. *My heart should be shattering.*

But her heart had shattered long ago, when she'd realized there was no future for her and the hottest cowboy to ever walk Diablo, New Mexico. Oh, she knew the ladies were gaga about the five other Callahan men, but in her opinion, only Peter Dade Callahan made her heart jump for joy every time she heard his name, saw his face, felt his hands on her.

Eventually, a girl had to move on with her life.

She grabbed her cell phone, dialed Darla. "I may run by and take a look at those papers again."

"I was hoping you'd be tempted," Darla told her.

"I just might be," Jackie said, listening as Pete's truck pulled from her drive. "I'll be there in a few minutes."

PETE THOUGHT HE WAS pretty good at reading women. In fact, there were times he'd thought he could write a book on the vagaries of the female mind.

Jackie had caught him so off guard he wondered how he could have missed the signs. Had he not just loved her within an inch of her life last Saturday night? She'd cried his name over and over so sweetly he'd been positive he had satisfied her every desire.

Now he was left to scratch at his five-o'-clock stubble with some puzzlement. Last Saturday night had been the last time he'd seen Jackie. He'd hidden his truck around back, as he always did. She liked to keep their relationship private, a plan he agreed with, thanks to the Diablo busybodies. Nobody wanted the Books 'n' Bingo ladies fastening their curiosity on them—it was a recipe for more well-meaning intrusion than a man could stand.

Jackie had cooked him dinner, and then, because she'd worked all day, he'd rented a movie, a chick flick. As the movie rolled, and guy got girl, Pete had massaged Jackie, starting with her shell-shaped toes, the delicate arches of her darling feet, then had even bent over to plant tender kisses on her ankles. The flower-patterned sofa in front of her TV was soft and puffy, a veritable haven of girliness, and he loved sitting there on Saturday nights like an old-fashioned date.

Then he always carried Jackie into her white-lace bedroom, his angel ensconced in gentle frills and woman's adornments, and he made love to her with a passion that he felt from the bottom of his heart.

In his mind, there was nothing better than Saturday nights with Jackie. It was so much a part of his routine—their routine—that he wasn't sure how he could live without it.

Apparently, she thought she could.

His heart felt as if it had been kicked.

He parked his truck and went inside the house. Aunt Fiona looked at him, her Cupid's-bow mouth making an O. "You're home quite early, Pete."

"Change of plans," he said, not about to share any details. Anyway, there was nothing to share. No one knew about him and Jackie, so there was nobody he could tell about the breakup, even if he wanted some sympathy, which he damn well didn't.

He wanted a handle of whiskey and a quiet room in which to nurse his pain.

"Did something happen?" Fiona asked.

"Like what?" he asked, rummaging through the liquor cabinet. Damn if he knew where Burke kept the goods.

"I don't know," Fiona said. "I just don't think I've ever seen you home at this hour on a Saturday night. Probably not in five years—ohhh."

He stopped moving bottles, pulled his head from the cabinet again. "What 'ohhh'?"

"Nothing. Nothing at all." Fiona went back to crocheting something that looked like a tiny white Christmas stocking.

He stared at her creative project, perplexed. "Are you making a *baby bootie?*"

She shoved the white thing into a basket at her feet. "Pete, if you're going to come home early on a Saturday night, that's your choice. But that doesn't mean you have the right to poke your nose into my business."

His jaw went slack. Nosiness wasn't something he'd been accused of before. He was known for being close-mouthed, secretive, even aloof. If Fiona was making baby booties, it was none of his business.

Yet, perhaps it was. Baby booties meant that Fiona had a taker for her plan. And that was a problem for him, because he wanted Rancho Diablo, and the woman he'd figured was a surefire deal had just given him the brush-off.

"Who are you making it for, Aunt Fiona?"

She cleared her throat. Got to her feet, sending him a cool, none-of-your-business stare worthy of a general. She took her basket and disappeared down the hall.

Pete lost his desire to drink. He shut the cabinet, then after a moment, left the house.

He felt lost in a way that he never had in his entire life. His woman had just left him; what would he do if he lost his home as well?

There was only one thing to do: He had to drive to Monterrey and watch the rodeo. Gamble a little, sing some karaoke, maybe let a sweet cowgirl calm his broken heart for the night. Chat with some buddies, go to cowboy church tomorrow morning—and then maybe this terrible problem would have gone away.

Maybe.

"COME TO BED, MY IRISH KNIGHT," Fiona said two hours later when Burke came into the bedroom they shared clandestinely.

"My wild Irish rose," Burke said, taking off his long coat and cold-weather cap. "I've been thinking."

"Think quietly, husband," Fiona said. "Pete came home tonight. We don't know where he might be lurking."

Burke glanced up as he stripped off the corduroy trousers he wore to oversee the locking-up of the old English-style house. A manor, her brother Jeremiah had wanted, just like the ones he'd seen in England before he'd had money. So that was what he'd built.

Jeremiah hadn't lived here long.

"Why is Peter here?" Burke asked.

"My uncomfortable suspicion is that he and Jackie may have had a wee falling-out."

Burke put on a robe made of Scottish wool and sank into his comfy leather armchair in front of the fireplace and directly across from the bed where his wife looked darling in her frilly white nightcap and flannel nightgown. "He said nothing?"

"No. But Pete's been the soul of discretion about his Saturday nights for so many years." Fiona sighed. "He wouldn't be here if something unfortunate hadn't occurred between them." Fiona hoped her pronouncement about the ranch hadn't stirred some sort of disagreement between them. Privately, she'd had her money on either Pete or Jonas to be the first to the altar. Stubborn Jonas had shocked her by walking away from the deal stone-cold. Now Pete might not be in quite the position she'd hoped he was in for a small nudge toward marriage. That left Creed and Rafe, Judah and Sam—none of whom she'd put a long bet on.

"Then I may have other bad news," Burke said, taking out his pipe carved from burled Irish wood. "All the other boys are in the bunkhouse."

"All the boys?" Fiona sat up straighter. "They're never home on Saturday nights! This is our night!"

"Be that as it may," Burke said, "they're engaged in a game of poker in the main bunkhouse." He drew with satisfaction on the pipe, then leaned over to stoke the fire.

"Burke! How can you be so calm! They're supposed to be competing against each other for Rancho Diablo!"

Burke smiled. "You've done an admirable job with the boys, Fiona. Now it's our turn. As I said, I've been thinking."

"Thinking about what?" Fiona didn't want to take her mind off her charges—although they weren't really her charges anymore, she supposed. They were full-grown men, responsible for their own happiness.

Still, the only way a man was happy—truly happy—was with a woman. Look at Burke, after all. He was the happiest man she'd ever met. Fiona smiled with satisfaction. Of course, he'd always said he preferred his creature comforts of home and hearth.

Her nephews didn't seem to share that opinion. They were more the type to fly the coop. Where had she gone wrong with them? Had she not been the best mother figure she knew how to be? And Burke...well, Burke had done as she'd asked. He'd remained a butler, not a stand-in father figure, which she thought the boys might have resented. They'd kept their marriage secret in order that the boys would always know that they were first priority for her, first in her heart. That she had done for her younger brother, Jeremiah, and his wife, Molly, a promise kept she'd never regretted.

"Let's renew our vows," Burke said. "I ask you, my love, to marry me in front of the whole town. Your Books 'n' Bingo ladies can be your bridesmaids."

Fiona stared. If Burke had suggested that the answer to their dilemma was for her to sprout wings and fly, she couldn't have been more shocked. She'd be more likely to sprout angel's wings because the man was about to give her heart failure.

Burke looked so earnest, with his bright-blue eyes and ruddy cheeks framed by very un-butlerish longish white hair, that she didn't dare stamp on his romantic tendencies, however much she felt that he wasn't thinking about her problem very seriously.

"Burke, we can't do that. You know I promised Jeremiah and Molly that I would see their boys to adulthood."

"And you've done that admirably." Burke smiled at her. "Sometimes I just sit and chuckle about how skillfully you've played your hand with those ruffians, Fiona."

"But they aren't married. They have no children. And have you forgotten, most importantly, that Rancho Diablo is going to be sold?"

This was the part that frightened her the most; the nightmare that kept her awake at night. She had failed Jeremiah. The castle of his dreams, the home where he and Molly had imagined raising their sons, wasn't really hers to raffle off to the brothers as she'd claimed. "Burke, they simply have to focus on their lives."

"Fiona," he said, getting up to lie on the bed with her, cradling her head to his chest, "they *are* concentrating on their lives."

"They'll hate me for losing the ranch."

"No."

"In a year, when it's all over, and the Callahan name is nothing but synonymous with a joke and pity—"

"Fiona, you sell these boys short. Anyway, they're not

even boys anymore. They're full-grown men. Why not just tell them the truth, instead of forcing them to find brides they may not want?"

"And the secret at the bottom of the stairs?" She looked up at her husband. "What do we do about that? And about their parents? Do you suggest I tell them that Jeremiah and Molly are still alive as well?"

Burke laid his pipe on the nightstand tray next to him and stroked his wife's head. "You worry too much, Fiona. It will all work out."

He'd always said that. She wasn't convinced this time. Rancho Diablo was in trouble. She could tell the brothers, see if they could raise enough money to somehow buy it back. Once they found out she'd put it up as a guarantee for a deal that had gone south, they might be able to do something. She probably owed it to them to tell them what had happened.

She couldn't. They couldn't help, she knew. And Jonas already had his eye on another property due east of here. He said he wanted his own place. Sympathy was her last card—community sympathy against that evil Bode Jenkins, their neighbor, and the scurvy bounder who'd convinced his daughter, the Honorable Judge Julie Jenkins, to cast their ranch as payment for the deal she'd greatly underestimated. Plus she owed a fearsome amount of taxes on a property that wouldn't be theirs in another year.

No one knew yet—but it would hit the grapevine soon enough. Fiona wasn't certain how much longer she could keep the dam from breaking. Her friends would always be her friends, but the boys—the boys she'd pledged to raise—stood to lose everything.

"Damn Bode Jenkins," Fiona said. "He outfoxed

me good this time. I wish he'd...I wish he'd fall into a river."

"Fiona," Burke murmured, patting his wife's head as she started to cry against his chest, "the boys are always going to love you."

She wished she could be certain of that.

Chapter Four

The bunkhouse door blew open. All five brothers glanced up. Snow and frigid wind blasted in with Jonas, who stamped his feet on the outside mat before closing the door.

"Look what the bad weather brought in," Pete said. "Couldn't make it to the airport?"

"Had no intention of leaving."

Pete took Jonas's coat and hung it on the hook in the entryway. His brother looked tired. "So where the hell have you been?"

"Following Miss Cavuti or whatever the hell her name was."

"You mean Madame Vivant. Sabrina McKinley." Pete chuckled. "I figured you had an eye for her."

"I do. And you should, too. Two eyes, in fact." Jonas glared at Pete, then around at the other brothers who sat on the dark-brown leather sectional, watching them. "Am I the only one who thought her story sounded odd?"

Sam shrugged. "Aunt Fiona can take care of herself. And Burke wouldn't let her come to any harm."

Pete applauded their youngest brother's common sense. Pete hadn't foreseen Jonas being so suspicious that he might follow the fortune-teller—if that's what she really was. Truthfully, Jonas was right to be suspicious, but he'd be better off putting all the suspicion on their dear Aunt Fiona.

Pete slapped Jonas on the back. "Well, join us for poker, bro. I'll grab you a beer, if you want."

Jonas shook his head. "No. All I want is some hot, black-as-night, stand-a-spoon-in-it coffee. It was colder and the snow was higher where those gypsies are now. I about froze my tail off."

"Where's their next stop?" Rafe asked.

"North of here. Buzzard's Peak or something like that. Think they're on their way to Montana." Jonas drank from the steaming mug Pete handed him.

"What makes you think they're headed to Montana?" Creed asked.

"They stopped at a truck stop to fill up." Jonas sank into the leather sofa with a sigh of appreciation to be home. "I got out to refuel, and spoke to one of the drivers."

"Sabrina didn't see you?" Rafe asked.

Jonas shook his head. "No. I'm sure she was bundled inside somewhere, counting whatever money she got from Fiona."

Pete smirked and reached for the cards. "Fiona wouldn't part with much hard-earned cash, Jonas."

His brother eyed him. The other men sat silently, waiting. It was not unusual for Jonas and Pete to have a difference of opinion. They were fifty-fifty on the outcome, Pete thought with satisfaction. And this time, he was holding all the cards.

"All I know," Jonas said, "is that Fiona's up to something. That bit about us getting married and having a bunch of kids is a smokescreen for something bigger."

Judah took the cards from Pete and began to deal. "Like what?"

"That's what I aim to find out." Jonas set his mug down and rubbed his hands. "I'm starting to thaw."

"Listen," Pete said, "Fiona has always looked out for our best interests. Why be so suspicious, Jonas?"

Jonas glared at him. "Why wouldn't she just divide the ranch between us, if it's simply a matter of her needing to write a will? All of us are financially capable. It's not like she's having to protect the ranch from us doing something stupid with it. I'm not saying that I want Rancho Diablo, particularly, but it is home. And I have to wonder why Fiona just didn't offer it to us and let us decide, instead of making us play marriage roulette for it. It bothers the hell of out me."

The brothers sat lost in their own thoughts, the only noise the popping of the roaring log fire. Pete wondered whether Jonas was so sore because he was the only one of them who'd once been within a foot of a wedding altar, then decided it was typical of Jonas to look out for the rest of them.

Pete studied his brother. "Jonas, we can decide whether to do this Fiona's way or not. You don't have to big-brother us anymore."

"Yeah?" Jonas glanced up, spearing his brother with a frosty gaze. "So how's finding a bride going to fit into your Saturday-night routine with Jackie Samuels, Pete?"

The brothers snickered. Pete thought about socking Jonas a good one, right in the nose, but it wouldn't solve anything, because Jonas was right.

He sighed. "Not too damn good."

"Jackie said no?" Sam asked.

"Look," Pete said, "no one's even supposed to know about Jackie and me, okay? So I don't really feel like discussing it."

"Dang," Creed said, "we all figured you'd be first to the altar. Then the rest of us would be off the hook."

Pete's brows went up in disbelief. "How would that work?"

"You'd get married, and we'd keep working the ranch, just like we do. Of course, we'd have to beat the hell out of you until you went to a lawyer and divided the ranch up between all of us." Rafe grinned. "That was the plan, anyway."

"Let me get this straight," Pete said, his tone as sour as his gut had suddenly become, "you wanted me to be the fall guy in this deal. As soon as the ranch was out of Fiona's control, you were going to highjack me into splitting it up between all of us."

"That's right," Sam said, "and it was a helluva good plan. We didn't count on you muffing the proposal to Jackie, though."

"Probably should have," Creed said. "If I'd bet a fiver on that, I'd be money-up right now."

Pete sank back into the sofa. "Here I thought I was doing a deal on you, and you were plotting against me and my new bride and family. You're a bunch of jackasses."

"What's that?" Judah said. "Did you say *we're* a bunch of jackasses?" He smirked at his brothers. "Who wants to hold Pete's head in a bucket of snow until he confesses?"

The brothers rose like a well-muscled, united wave. Pete put up a hand of surrender. "Calm down. All I was keeping from you—and it's just a small thing, nothing like what you were up to—"

"We'll decide that by family vote," Jonas said, "don't leave out any of the details."

Pete was torn. He hated to blow up Aunt Fiona's

excellent plan. On the other hand, Jonas had a great point. Maybe the fortune-teller *had* done something to Fiona's mind. He had no idea, after all, exactly how much coin had changed hands. There'd been no sign outside the tent at the fair indicating a fee for services.

"Pete," Sam said, his voice deep with warning. "Don't sit there and concoct a story, or we will hold you in censure."

That was bad. Last time one of them had been censured by the other brothers, Rafe—the unlucky bastard—had had his face tattooed in his sleep by a nice, usually calm lady—Judge Julie Jenkins next door. Rafe had been done in by his own twin, as Creed had opened the door for Julie. She'd brought an indelible red-ink pen, and the brothers had merely guffawed as she approached Rafe, who had crashed on the sofa. Rafe had been on a bender, so he hadn't noticed until he'd gotten up the next morning to go to Mass and had found himself looking like something out of a girlie revenge flick. His entire face had been covered with tiny hearts, probably fifty of them.

Julie was no pushover, and she thought Rafe was an ass. He hadn't tried to get smart with that little lady twice. Pete winced when he thought about Rafe scrubbing his face for days after Julie's sneak attack. Fiona had given Rafe some rubbing alcohol, but in the end, only time had worn away the tiny hearts on his face. His brothers had ribbed him for days, and Rafe had been unable to leave the ranch for the sake of machismo. If Rafe hadn't been in a state of censure with his brothers, they would never have let a miffed female in to pen her revenge on his face. They would have at least stopped her at five, maybe ten, hearts. They'd never asked Rafe what had gotten him crosswise with Julie, and he'd never offered any information. Pete wasn't eager to suffer a similar fate. "Fiona hired Sabrina to tell us the ranch was in trouble."

"Hired her?" Judah repeated. "Madame Vivant didn't work a nefarious plan on her?"

Pete shook his head. "Nope. I'm sure Fiona's as right in her mind as any of us. No one would ever take advantage of her. Not easily, anyway." He looked at his brothers' incredulous faces. "I feel bad ratting out her plan."

The poker game was abandoned. They were in a bigger game now, Pete thought. "At the time, I thought it was funny. She was trying to maneuver us into settling down. I had a girlfriend already, so it wasn't—"

"You were going to cheat us," Creed said. "You were getting a head start."

"No—" Pete began, then he slumped in the sofa. "Yeah."

They considered him with disapproving expressions.

"It's no different from you thinking you had me set up to fall first, thereby letting you off the hook," Pete said in defense of himself. "And I didn't feel that it was any of my business to spoil Fiona's plan."

"This is true," Sam said, "but we've always known we had to look out for each other."

Pete sighed. "Oh, shut the hell up. None of you wants to get married anyway. So don't act like you could have caught up with me if Jackie had said yes."

"Assuming you're not shooting blanks," Jonas said darkly. "Five years of dating is an awful lot of raincoats. I've never seen you make a run to the drugstore."

Pete felt a flush run up his neck. "There's nothing

wrong with my gun, thanks. Jackie's probably on the pill or something."

Sam's mouth fell open. "You never asked her?"

"Hell, no. She's a nurse. What could I tell a nurse about birth control?" Now that his brothers were ribbing him about it, though, Pete wondered. He'd never seen anything in Jackie's house that looked like birth control pills. In fact, he'd never known her even to take cold medicine. She was a big believer in homeopathy, when appropriate, and eating healthy like a granola-starved hippie. Fresh food was the key to life, she'd say, setting a snack in front of him, and he'd smile and eat and mostly stare at her, not caring if she fed him dirt so long as he got into the sack with her.

"Damn, you're not much of a stud," Judah said, "if you don't even know whether you should be wrapping up."

Pete jumped to his feet. "There is nothing wrong with my—with me! I could have children if I wanted them, if Jackie wanted them." He didn't know if she did, but he wasn't going to admit that. Now that he thought about it, he and Jackie hadn't done a whole lot of talking about big life issues.

"Sit down. We're just trying to figure out what to do here." Jonas shoved him back down into the sofa, with a determined thrust that collapsed Pete. He felt as though his world was spinning, anyway. Did Jackie want children? He assumed that particular desire was baked into the DNA of all women. "Anyway, I never got around to asking her to marry me. She—" He took a painful swallow of beer. "She ran me off."

They took that in for a minute with an assortment of grunts and empathetic groans.

"Sorry about Jackie," Sam said. "Sucks, dude."

Pete glanced up at the first vote of sympathy he'd heard from his brothers, realizing how much he appreciated the sentiment. His other brothers reached over and either clouted him on the back or punched him in the arm. He felt better, as much as he possibly could, under the circumstances. "Guess you'll need a different plan."

"It just doesn't make sense." Jonas glanced around at his brothers. "There has to be something pushing Fiona to be this drastic. I had my doubts about that little con artist she brought in, figured she'd at least hang around to try to worm something out of Fiona or the ranch, but she seems to have been happy to take her fee and go." He squinted at Pete. "Why the hell were you going to let us all get caught in a noose, bro, if you knew it was a set-up?"

Pete shrugged. "Wouldn't kill any of us to settle down."

"Might kill me," Sam said. "I live a monklike existence."

This earned hoots from his brothers. Pete rolled his eyes. "Anyway, I thought it was kind of cute to hear Fiona and her bingo buddies trying to put one over on us. I figured I was pulling one over on her by hearing her plans."

"But still," Rafe said, "you planned to have the jump on us since you already had a woman picked out. I don't know if I feel good about that."

"I had a girl picked out," Pete said, trying not to wince, "but who knows if she would have wanted children immediately? These things take two people, and all the decision wasn't mine. So I was only ahead in the fact that I had a woman I thought I had a relationship with."

"Oh, I don't care about any of that," Judah said, pulling out his wallet. "I think I've got some hot-date phone numbers in here from the last rodeo. I can probably catch up pretty quick, if you guys want to let Fiona think her plan is succeeding. What does it hurt to give her a little pleasure?"

Creed shook his head. "I say we go to Fiona and tell her we're all joining the priesthood. That'll frost her."

Pete laughed, then straightened. "No! We can't give her any reason to suspect that we know anything."

Jonas looked at him. "We can't decide our futures based on emergency trips to the marriage license office."

"Do you currently base your future on more sound decisions than what Fiona has suggested?" Pete looked around the room at his siblings. "I don't think any of you realize this, but Fiona wasn't just our guardian. She wasn't just a parent. She keeps a lot of secrets in her drive to be our number-one protector and cheerleader."

Sam laughed. "You make it sound like she and her little friends sit around and plot all day."

Pete nodded. "Don't kid yourself. That's exactly what she does."

They went silent again. The wind howled outside, picking up a violent sound. Pete wondered if he should drag one of his brothers out with him to check on the cattle and the horses. The wind whipped so hard over their bunkhouse that it reminded him of crying ghosts, something he'd always wondered about when he was a child. He'd always felt that ghosts lived just as freely at Rancho Diablo as the Callahans did.

Maybe the ghosts hung around because they liked it here. Pete was determined to feel positive about anything he could concerning Rancho Diablo.

"Let's make a pact," Sam said suddenly. "One of us—whoever can do it first—will get married. Try to have kids. The rest of us will be hellaciously good uncles."

Everyone stared at Sam.

"Since you're only twenty-six," Jonas said, his tone wry, "that almost makes your suggestion a bit callous."

Sam shook his head. "I might have my eye on a gal. You don't know."

Pete sighed. "He may have a point. Only one is needed for sacrificial-lamb status, as long as everyone agrees that once Fiona has given the ranch over to us, we formally split ownership in a lawyer's office."

"It's a bad idea between brothers," Judah said. "Not that I don't trust all of you, but Fiona is trying to play us off against each other. No telling what rabbit she might pull out of her hat next." He looked at Pete. "Besides, you seem to know more about her than the rest of us. These secrets she's keeping that you're hinting at—are they as much of a hairball as her marriage-and-kids plot? 'Cause while I trust everyone in this room, I'm not sure if you deserve trust, Pete, considering."

"He's right," Jonas said. "You seem to have information that could affect the rest of us."

"No," Pete said, "I mean, I just know her too well. Fiona works constantly on our behalf. All I meant was that she…she keeps things to herself." He was uncomfortable under his brothers' laser scrutiny. There wasn't a whole lot of trust being beamed at him.

"Can you give us an example?" Creed asked. "I'm getting mighty pissed about all the secrecy surrounding what should be my life."

"I don't know what all she keeps under her hat," Pete said, becoming defensive and somewhat hostile himself. "The only thing I know for sure is that she and Burke are married. And that's not such a big secret, is it?" Pete looked at all his brothers for confirmation that the bombshell he'd just dropped was, in fact, just a tiny one.

Five faces glared at him.

"Fiona is married to the butler, and you didn't tell us?" Jonas demanded. "Are you insane? When did this happen? You don't think this affects our futures?"

"Not really," Pete said, feeling his hackles rise. "They did it about a hundred years ago, for crying out loud. I found the marriage certificate when I was digging around in the cabinets in the basement."

"Holy crow," Sam said, "you should've been a spy."

"You sorry sack of crap," Creed said, "why'd you keep that under your hat?"

Rafe looked shocked. Judah looked as though he might take a swing at something, chiefly Pete.

"Look," he said to Jonas, feeling that his eldest brother was the only one in the room who might defend him, "it was none of our business if she didn't want us to know."

"I don't know," Creed muttered, "seems like you've appointed yourself the keeper of the family secrets."

"Not so much," Pete said, "considering we've never known that much about our family anyway."

Chapter Five

After a few moments of stunned silence, Jonas said, "We've done enough talking, at least in my opinion. We're just getting mad, and we need to be focused on what to do about Fiona."

Obviously, any discussion of their family history was off the table. Pete was okay with that. He hadn't wanted to talk about Fiona anyway. Or their troubled family tree. "Suits me, if anybody has a game plan."

"No," Sam said, his voice quiet. "We can't do anything until we talk to Fiona."

"No," Pete said. "We can't let her know that we're on to her. She works so hard to wrangle us in the direction she thinks is right for us. And you know, a lot of times, that little aunt of ours has been right."

They digested that. Jonas poked at the fire again. Sparks erupted with a pop and a log crashed to the bottom of the grate. Judah squatted in front of the fireplace to toss in a couple of logs. Overhead a fan swirled in a lazy motion, keeping the air stirred. Family photos lined the mantel, mostly black-and-white memories of the brothers. Fiona loved to take pictures of them. She was good with a camera and had captured their growing-up years with skill. Under the sofa, a hand-worked rug by a Native American artisan warmed the stone floor.

Other decor they'd picked up on jaunts into Santa Fe graced the large, beam-ceilinged room, mementoes of what Fiona called family getaways. She'd bought a van, the biggest one she could find, and all the boys and Burke would pile in while Fiona drove them all over the Southwest once a year. She'd been a great parent. Pete swallowed. He didn't want her feelings hurt. "Look, let's just forget about it, okay? None of us want to get married, not really. So it doesn't matter."

"Yeah, so what happens to the ranch if something happens to Fiona?" Rafe asked. "She said she hasn't been feeling well."

Jonas sat up. "I'll check on her tomorrow."

"Rafe's right." Creed brought the coffeepot and a plate of cookies Fiona had left in the kitchen over to the table. "Anything could happen. We're going to have to ask her."

"You ask her, Jonas," Pete said.

His older brother shook his head. "No. We'll have a family meeting at the appropriate time."

"In the spring," Pete said. "It doesn't matter right now, does it? Christmas vacation doesn't seem like the time to bring up family issues."

"It's the third of January. Technically, vacation is over. And she started the discussion," Sam reminded him. "She brought in the fortune-teller."

That was true. There was no defense Pete could offer. "I wish I hadn't said anything."

"You know what I wonder," Sam said, ignoring Pete's doubts, "is where our parents really are."

All six brothers sat like stone statues, cookies left on the tray, seconds ticking loudly on the mantel clock. Pete felt hair stand up on the back of his neck as regret washed over him. He'd opened up a box of trouble with his tale of Fiona's plot to make them family men. "Our parents are buried somewhere in a graveyard, Sam."

Jonas looked at Sam. Sam stared back at Jonas.

"Go ahead. Say it," Sam said. "I know what you're thinking."

Jonas jumped to his feet, paced the room. Turned away from the brothers. Scrubbed at his chin, took a deep breath. Pete wondered what the hell was going on. He felt deep waters eddying around them and hoped they weren't all going to drown. Something was going terribly wrong in the family—and it had to do with Rancho Diablo.

"I'm not so sure our parents are buried anywhere," Jonas said, as he turned back around. "We've never seen their graves."

Judah blinked. "Did we ever ask?"

Pete shook his head. "I didn't. Why would Fiona tell us they'd died if they hadn't? Why did she and Burke come from Ireland to raise us if they weren't gone?" A bad feeling wrapped itself around Pete, a question that had always been at the back of his mind but which he'd ignored. Wanted to ignore still.

"What Jonas isn't saying," Sam said, "is that I came later. And he remembers it."

They all looked from Jonas to Sam. Pete felt a snake of worry start in the pit of his stomach, pulling tight.

"So that's why he thinks our parents might not be deceased," Sam said. "And that's why he's suspicious about Fiona cooking up a plan to have us compete for the ranch." Sam looked at Jonas. "Right? That's why you really followed Madame Vivant?"

Pete crossed to the window, staring into the darkness, feeling the cold pane against his forehead. Nothing good was going to come of this night, and he wished he'd kept his big mouth shut. He and his brothers had always been close but reserved, keeping to themselves a lot.

He felt further apart from his brothers than ever.

There was a cauldron of family secrets stewing away—they all kept them. It protected them somehow from the underlying sense of not-quite-normal that surrounded the ranch. He glanced up at the moon—a fat, round harbinger of time. No one had yet mentioned the old Navajo who arrived like clockwork every year on the night before Christmas. He and Fiona went to the basement and stayed for an hour, and they had no idea why. Burke always sat with the brothers in the library, keeping them busy with conversation and cookies when they were young, and later with whiskey and a list of items he said needed to be conquered at the ranch. They'd always thought of this as their yearly Burke business meeting, their chance to help out Fiona and Burke with the running of the ranch. Now Pete realized Burke had merely been keeping them busy, away from the real business which was being conducted underneath the house.

Something was going on, something that had to do with Fiona's sudden desire that they settle down. Pete thought about Jackie, wondered what she was doing, debated whether she'd mind a late Saturday-night visitor, even though she'd just sent him away.

He felt certain she hadn't changed her mind in the few hours since he'd left her place. Probably she hadn't, but as the snow swirled outside and his brothers mused about Callahan family problems, Pete made a break for freedom.

"I'm going out," he said, jamming his hat on his head and buckling up a long oilskin coat.

"Bad night for it," Sam warned. "Could be snow drifts as high as your ass."

"It's okay," Pete said, "I'm already in up to my ass. Can't get any worse."

He hurried to the barn, checked the horses and saddled Bleu, a huge black stallion suited to riding over snow and ice. Didn't panic easily. Kind of like Pete, who hated dark emotion and stress—he wanted nothing more at this moment than to get away from a rising sense of panic he couldn't explain.

HE TAPPED ON JACKIE'S front door after noting that her car was parked alongside the house. Dangerous, thanks to the snow. He'd advise her to put it away, or do it for her if she wanted.

She came to the door, her expression curious and not necessarily pleased. "Pete! What are you doing here?"

He wished he'd ignored his urge to see her at all costs—he felt unwelcome, worse than he had back at the bunkhouse with his brothers.

"Come in," she said. "Tie Bleu under the eaves."

Usually she said, *Put Bleu in the barn,* so there wasn't a chance he was being asked to resume their comfortable Saturday-night routine. Bleu had been tied under the eaves before and he'd be fine, but it was going to be a quick visit, in this cold weather. "I won't be long," he muttered to Bleu, "so don't give me that face."

The horse blew out his disdain for being treated like a common yard ornament. "Sorry," Pete told him, "this is important."

He went inside, staying at the front door on the pretty floral rug. "You're all dressed up," he said, surprised that she wasn't in her nightgown at this hour. *Old routine,* he reminded himself. *Back when we were us.* The black dress and boots she wore made him realize how much he was going to miss her in his life.

Well, it didn't take a dress and boots for Jackie to be hot, but he realized how many times he'd taken her out on a date. *Zero.*

"What can I do for you, Pete?"

He gazed into her dark-chocolate eyes, feeling as if he were drowning. *Say you didn't mean to send me out of your life. That it was all a mistake.*

"I'm not sure. I just wanted to see you." That sounded so lame he frowned. "Wanted to check on you."

That didn't sound any better. Jackie shook her head. "I'm fine, as you can see."

Great. Here he stood, a giant useless doofus, taking up her time when she clearly had some place to go. "Jackie—"

"I'm sorry, Pete." She did look regretful, which helped somewhat. "I have an appointment. You caught me just as I was leaving."

An appointment at eight o'clock at night? That was a polite way of saying she had a date. There was nothing else Jackie could be doing looking as hot as she did.

Pete had no idea how their steady relationship had jumped the tracks as it had.

"Okay. Thanks." He drank in her heart-shaped face, the slight confusion that lifted her dark brows. She really didn't understand why he'd come. Didn't feel the same things he did. "Good night, Jackie."

"Good night, Pete."

She watched him go out the door and untie Bleu. He swung up into the saddle, glancing back at her. She stood under the porch light, her arms wrapped around herself, the way his arms wanted to be. Needed to be.

He felt too helpless to do more than wave a hand at her to say goodbye. The gesture felt more like surrender. She waved back, and he rode away, which also felt like surrender.

JACKIE WATCHED PETE disappear into the night, Bleu anxious to be off again as Pete gave him free rein. She closed the door, her heart heavy. Maybe she wasn't making the right decision. Pete had been her guy for so long it was hard to think about him never holding her in his arms again.

"Change is necessary," she reminded herself. "We weren't going anywhere."

A knock on the front door filled her heart with a sense of hope that shouldn't be there—but it was. "Pete?" she said, opening the door.

A woman stood on her porch. She looked cold, her reddish hair shining under the porch light, her nose pink from the harsh conditions.

"Can I help you?" Jackie asked, now wishing she hadn't answered the knock.

"I'm sorry to bother you this late," her visitor said. Her green eyes expressed true remorse at the intrusion. Jackie held her breath as a strange chill passed over her. "This is awkward," her guest continued, "but Fiona Callahan sent me."

Jackie blinked. "Why?"

"She said you might want to talk to me." The woman shrugged delicate shoulders that were covered by a black wool poncho. "My name is Sabrina McKinley. I'm a fortune-teller with the circus that just came through town."

"You don't really tell fortunes?"

"I tell people what they want to hear."

Why would Fiona send a charlatan to her? "I don't need to hear anything. But thank you for stopping by."

She started to close the door, hesitating when Sabrina spoke.

"Children are a blessing," Sabrina said. "You have been blessed three times."

I don't want to hear this. This woman knows nothing about my life. "I'm sorry," Jackie said. "I don't mean to be rude, but I have an appointment, and—"

"It's all right," Sabrina said. "Can you tell me how to get to Bode Jenkins's house?"

"Bode Jenkins?" Jackie took a more thorough look at her visitor. "Why do you want to go there, if you don't mind me asking?"

"Fiona thinks he might need to talk." Sabrina shrugged, the poncho moving gracefully as she did.

Bode didn't talk to anyone, not much anyway. He'd eat this tiny woman alive for showing up on his porch. Yet, it wasn't her place to interfere. "Can I ask you a question?"

Sabrina smiled. "People usually do."

"Oh. Right. No, I meant…did you tell something to Fiona?"

"Client confidentiality," Sabrina said. "I'm sure you understand."

"Absolutely." Jackie didn't. On the other hand, she wouldn't want this woman talking about whatever she knew about her.

Oh, baloney. This lady knows nothing about me. It's all hogwash.

Sabrina stepped away from the door. "It was nice meeting you."

Jackie stared after her as she went down the porch steps and crunched off in the snow, leaving tracks with her small boots. Why was Fiona mixed up with a gypsy?

"I—" Jackie told herself not to get involved. Yet a visitor could get lost around here when she didn't know her way, especially with snow obscuring everything. She was going to be totally late to Darla's, but did it matter? Talking about the wedding business could wait thirty more minutes. "If you follow me, I'll take you by the entrance to the Jenkins's ranch."

"Thanks." Sabrina smiled. "The new business is a great idea, by the way. You should always follow your heart."

Once again, chills ran over Jackie that weren't weather-related. She decided to ignore Sabrina's words—maybe Darla had mentioned it to Fiona, who'd told Sabrina—but at the same time, she couldn't help but feel that the wind was blowing just a bit colder. She hurried to the car. "I'll drive slowly, so you don't lose sight of my taillights."

Nodding, Sabrina got into her truck. It was an old one, a white Ford that had seen better days. Jackie shook her head and started her own car—and felt the strangest jump in her stomach. A flutter, like a butterfly moving across her abdomen.

She glanced out at the horizon, and her breath caught. Black horses ran across the horizon, tails and manes flying. It was beautiful and mystical, and Jackie suddenly thought about the black Diablos. But it couldn't be them. She was a good twenty miles away from Pete's ranch. And though Pete swore they were real, everyone else thought they were a myth dreamed up by the crazy Callahans. Fey Fiona and her Irish tales.

The wild hoofbeats she was hearing were nothing more than her own blood pounding in her ears.

Chapter Six

"She kind of wigged me out." Jackie glanced at Darla thirty minutes later as she sat in her friend's living room sipping hot tea. Their business papers were spread out on the table in front of her, but Jackie couldn't stop thinking about Sabrina McKinley. "I've never talked to a fortune-teller before. I don't know why it spooked me."

"I wonder at Fiona for sending her to your house," Darla said. "No matter. You got her to Bode's, and I feel bad enough for her having to pay a call on that troll."

Jackie looked down into her cup. She did, too. "So, where do we start?"

"Here are some ideas on financing. Here is the new spring inventory that has already been bought for next year." Darla pointed to different papers. "Best of all, here are the orders that are outstanding already for next June. Who would have thought we had so many antsy brides around Diablo?"

It was almost like reading a gossip sheet. Jackie gasped as she looked down the list of names Darla gave her. "I didn't know all these people were engaged!"

"And lucky for us they are." Darla grinned. "Love is definitely in the air."

Jackie felt a shard of pain go through her. Love was in the air, but not for her. Pete did not love her. He was going through some break-up pangs, probably, but they would pass. She knew her guy. Pete lived in the moment. He didn't think about the future, or life beyond the next Saturday night.

She was the worrier, the seeker. "This is great. This is just what I need."

"Really?" Darla beamed. "I was hoping you'd say that! Let's break out some champagne, partner!"

Jackie smiled, then remembered the strange flutter in her stomach. "Maybe just a soda for me. I've got a bit of a nervous stomach tonight for some reason."

Darla peered at her. "Do you think you might have a bug? There's been a lot of flu going around the hospital."

"I don't think it's a bug." Jackie felt a bit peaked. "Is it warm in here to you?"

"I'm fine," Darla said. "Let's go in the kitchen and get you a cold drink."

Darla got up and Jackie followed, although not with any enthusiasm. She wasn't certain ice would be enough to make her feel better. "So, if we decide to buy the wedding boutique, when do you plan to turn in your resignation?"

"I already did." Darla plunked three cubes into a glass, filled it with ginger ale and handed it to Jackie. "I gave my two weeks' notice, and I'm happy to be free."

Jackie nodded. "I will be, too." She thought about Mr. Dearborn, who loved to stir her up. "I'll miss it, but I do need a break."

Darla smiled. "Are you and Pete having some kind of little romance problems?"

Jackie blinked. "Why?"

"Just checking. You seem a little out of sorts."

The warmth was definitely back, despite the ginger

ale, but this time it was embarrassment. "We broke up tonight."

"What happened?" Darla looked concerned. "This is a small town. You know better than to think you can keep something like that quiet around here. Tell me everything before I hear it through the grapevine."

Jackie shook her head. "How long has everyone known?"

"Since your mother told Fiona, and she told all her buddies at the Books 'n' Bingo Society. Which includes my mom." Darla grinned at her. "We've all known forever that you were sweet on each other."

"Why didn't you say anything?"

Darla shrugged. "I just thought you'd mention it to folks if you wanted to. Besides, it isn't like I don't know something about having a crush on a Callahan man."

"Really?" Jackie tried to picture Darla with any of the brothers and couldn't come up with one who could elude her gutsy, determined friend. "Who?"

"I'm going to wait five years to tell you, just like you did. Let's see if I can keep a secret that long," Darla teased.

"Tell me now."

Darla shook her head. "Unlike you, my secret crush has no idea I think he's a total stud. And we're going to keep it that way, unless I can figure out a spell to get him to notice me."

"I guess you could always ask Sabrina. She seems to know everything."

Darla glanced at her. "She really got to you, didn't she?"

Jackie perched on a bar stool at the counter. "She said I was going to be blessed with three children."

"Wow," Darla said, "that's better than a home pregnancy test." She giggled.

Jackie felt better just mentioning it. "Silly, huh?"

"Completely weird. Don't let it bother you."

"I'm not sure it altogether bothered me." Jackie looked at Darla, then smiled. "I felt sorry for her."

"She tells you you're going to have three kids, and you feel sorry for her? I'd be feeling sorry for myself."

"You don't want children?"

"If they were Judah's children, I'd have all he wanted." Darla grinned. "I could be a happy, barefoot and pregnant bride if the man involved was Judah Callahan."

"Judah! I should have known you'd fall for a hard case."

"I like a challenge, what can I say?" Darla smiled. "But unless it's with him, I won't be having children. I'm a career woman. I want to make enough money to buy my own tiny ranch." Darla looked around her house. "I love it here, but I want a place where I can have horses."

Jackie nodded. She understood. A Callahan man, a ranch, horses, children—wouldn't that just be heaven?

"So why'd you and Pete break up?" Darla asked. "You look so sad."

"I don't really want to talk about it." Jackie sipped at the ginger ale, feeling another squirm in her stomach. It was strange. She was never sick, never had aches and pains.

"You may not have a choice," Darla told her. "You looked sad when you came inside, and now you look like you've lost your dog. People will figure it out."

Jackie sighed. "We broke up because it wasn't going anywhere."

"Where did you want it to go?"

"Someplace different than Saturday-night sex."

"Oh. I suppose just asking for additional Monday-night sex was out of the question?"

Jackie smiled. "I don't know. We'd been in a routine for so long it had become a rut."

Darla looked at her. "How did Pete take the news?"

She remembered him standing on her porch, staring at her with hungry eyes. "He didn't say a whole lot."

"Typical Callahan."

Jackie felt another butterfly float across her stomach. "Listen, I think I'm going to head out. What papers do you want me to sign before I go?"

Darla grinned. "Several papers. And we'll need to go to the bank on Monday. But," she said with a teasing smile, "if the fortune-teller's right and you turn up pregnant, you have to model one of our gowns at your wedding."

"Oh, sure," Jackie said, "fat chance."

But deep inside her heart, Jackie knew she would have loved to have had a child with Pete. "Hey, let's take a drive."

"A drive where?" Darla asked.

"Over to the Jenkins'."

Darla hesitated before getting up to put her long blond hair into a ponytail. She pulled on a knitted cap and a wool jacket. "I'm ready to ride."

"You don't mind?"

"I totally understand. You'd feel better if you knew that Mr. Jenkins hadn't yelled three years off the life of your new friend. Or shot her." Darla shrugged and turned the lamps down. "The thought crossed my mind, too. She must have some strong magic or Fiona wouldn't have sent her to the bear's den."

Jackie got up to follow Darla to the door. "I don't

think she has any mystical powers at all. I think she's just one of Fiona's friends."

"That's not saying much. I'm one of Fiona's friends, or at least my mother is, and I don't have any powers. Shall we stop at the drug store on the way and pick up a test for you?"

"No, thanks."

"Wouldn't it be funny if the fortune-teller was right?"

"No," Jackie said, "it would not."

Ten minutes later, Jackie and Darla stood on Mr. Jenkins's porch, stamping their feet to get the snow off. They could see Sabrina's old truck in the gravel drive.

"I can see them through the window," Jackie said.

"Not that we should be spying, but scoot over so I can see." Darla stepped up to peer inside. "They look like they're having a friendly chat."

"Yeah." Jackie was surprised Bode Jenkins had let Sabrina into his house. He was known for being rude to visitors and stingy with his hospitality. "Are they drinking tea?"

"And eating brownies, I think. Those are Julie's brownies," Darla said. "I recognize the frosting on top and the tiny white chocolate chips. She gives them out every year for Christmas."

A flash of indigestion hit Jackie, surprising her. She, too, looked forward to the judge's brownies, so why had her stomach suddenly pitched?

Fear. "We should go," she murmured. "We don't want Mr. Jenkins to think we were—"

"Being nosey, which we are. Maybe we should ring the bell and see if we can get ourselves invited in for tea and one of those brownies, though."

"Hi, Jackie! Darla!"

Jackie swallowed a gasp, whirling. "Julie! Hi!"

Darla had jumped a foot beside her, but now all she said was, "Hi, Julie. We were just about to ring the bell."

Julie's brown eyes twinkled. "Come on in. Dad's got a visitor, but he won't mind a few more."

"We wouldn't want to bother anyone," Jackie said, and Darla said, "Sure, we could come inside for a minute."

"Let me help you with that firewood," Jackie murmured, taking a few sticks of it from Julie though the judge clearly had it handled.

Darla pulled the door open for Julie. "Was there anything special you were stopping by about?" Julie asked.

Darla's eyes met Jackie's. "We were going to get your thoughts on a business matter," Jackie said. "We should have called first."

"We always have visitors, and you're always especially welcome," Julie said, including both of them in her gracious words.

It was true. Julie did get lots of callers, mostly men who weren't afraid of Bode waving a shotgun at them. Cakes and pies were known to make their way with some frequency to the Jenkins's household, particularly if a grievance had been settled in someone's favor.

"Jackie, Darla, this is Sabrina McKinley," Julie said. "She's a home-care provider who's come to visit Dad. Please come in and sit down, and have some tea with us."

"Hello, Sabrina," Jackie said. Darla murmured a greeting as well. Sabrina smiled at them, and the indigestion Jackie was suffering turned up a notch. "Good evening, Mr. Jenkins."

"You're interrupting," Bode said. "Do you know what time it is? Past time for a social call!"

Jackie and Darla backtracked to the door. "You're absolutely right, Mr. Jenkins. We're so sorry. Julie, we'll call you tomorrow."

"You don't have to go—" Julie began, but Jackie already had the door open.

"Good night, all. It was good to see everyone," Jackie said.

"At least take some brownies with you," Julie said, holding out a napkin with two on it.

Darla snatched the brownies. "Thanks, Julie. We'll take you to lunch one day this week. Good night, everyone!"

They hurried to the truck. Jackie was out of breath after scrambling through the slushy snow. "Gosh! That's what we get for trying to busybody as successfully as Fiona!" Jackie cranked the ignition and gunned the truck down the snow-covered gravel drive.

"I thought you said Sabrina was just a garden-variety fortune-teller." Darla chewed her brownie happily. "These brownies are great. Are you going to want yours?"

"No." Nausea swept Jackie at the mention of food. "Maybe I am coming down with a bug."

"Perhaps we should carry a line of christening gowns, maybe even matching mom-and-me bride and baby gowns."

"I'm not pregnant," Jackie said, still thinking about Sabrina. Very tough to put anything over on Judge Julie. The home-health-care provider story was an angle Jackie hadn't envisioned.

"We'll see," Darla said. "Everybody's stories seem to be changing pretty fast. Good thing you're in the mood for change, huh?"

"Yeah," Jackie said, "I'm a real big fan of change."

ON SUNDAY MORNING, Pete noticed Fiona looked shocked—and none too pleased—when all of them piled into the van. This was nothing different from their usual routine. Whoever was available on Sunday mornings jumped in the van to go to Mass with Fiona and Burke.

"Good morning, Aunt Fiona, Burke," Pete said, as they all grabbed their usual seats.

She turned to glare at them. "What are you doing?"

"Keeping you company, just like we always do," Pete said, to a chorus of accompanying grunts from his brothers.

"You should be out looking for wives," she said, her doughy little face sweet—determined, yet sweet.

"Don't you worry about a thing, dear aunt." Pete patted her on the shoulder. "We've come up with a solution to the problem."

She brightened. "You have?" She cast a slightly optimistic glance over the carload of big men. "I'm so happy to hear it. Did you hear that, Burke? They have a solution!"

Burke started the engine. "Windshield wipers are stuck. Just a minute." He got out of the van.

"So tell me," Fiona said. "Don't make me wait."

"Sam's going to get married," Pete said.

Fiona's eyes went wide. "Sam?"

Sam nodded. "If it makes you happy, Aunt Fiona, it's no skin off my nose."

She glanced around the van. "Anybody else?"

"Nope," Pete said. "Sam's getting married, so Sam will get Rancho Diablo."

"You're all nutty as fruitcakes if you think I'm going to fall for this," Fiona said. "What a bunch of sissies!"

Pete blinked. "None of us, with the exception of Sam, are ready to settle down. So we forfeit."

Fiona turned back around. Pete could see her staring out the window, watching Burke as he picked ice off the wipers. "Well, then," she said, her tone deceptively enthusiastic, "whom are you going to marry, Sam?"

Pete glanced at Sam, as did all the other brothers. Fiona turned to pin her youngest nephew with a watchful look that was all Fiona. They'd seen that look too many times over the years not to heed the warning to tread carefully.

"Well, I—" Sam glanced around to his brothers for help. They hadn't planned that far into their scheme. Pete looked at Sam. Jonas sighed, rolling his eyes, which for some reason, seemed to force his youngest brother to a decision.

"I'm going to marry—" Sam gulped. "I thought I might ask Madame Vivant, er, Sabrina. It was love at first sight," he finished with a flourish.

The van went as silent as a coffin.

"Really?" Fiona asked. "Have you even talked to her, Sam? I thought she'd left town."

"No." He shook his head. "She was at Bode Jenkins's last night."

Now everyone stared at Sam.

"And you know this how?" Jonas asked. "I was up quite a bit north of here following their train, so I'm not sure how she could have been at Bode's."

"Oh, she was." Sam nodded enthusiastically. "I saw her go in, and when she left, I went out and talked to her."

Pete noticed Jonas getting real red around his fancy church-shirt collar. "I thought you were in the bunkhouse with us."

"I went out to check on the horses. Thought I heard something, got worried about wolves." Sam grinned. "And there she was, like Little Bo Peep who'd lost her way."

"Sheep, she's supposed to lose sheep," Pete said, not sure if his brother was embellishing the tale or not. All Sam was supposed to do was convince Fiona he intended to marry for the ranch. He was supposed to soothe Fiona.

What Sam was doing was making Jonas madder by the minute. Pete watched with great interest as Jonas's brows slid lower, practically pinching together.

"That woman is off limits," Jonas stated.

"Why?" Sam asked.

Burke got back into the van, letting in frigid air, but it couldn't have been any colder with the eldest and the youngest Callahans staring each other down.

"Because there's no such thing as love at first sight." Jonas stared out the window.

"Huh." Fiona turned around, clearly unimpressed. "Sounds like a fish tale to me. I'm not buying it, Samuel Callahan."

Sam glanced around at his brothers for help. Pete shrugged. "Don't look at me. I've got no girl to marry."

"Pitiful," Fiona said. "Just pitiful. Burke, hurry and get us to church. I'm no saint, and my patience is wearing thinner than it's ever been."

Sam and Jonas were still glaring at each other. Creed and Rafe stared out opposite windows, and Judah looked as though he couldn't care less about the whole scheme.

Pete shrugged again, about to suggest that they go into town for pancakes after church—just to change the subject to a topic less likely to inflame the entire family—when he saw a familiar truck pull into their driveway.

"Oh, look," Fiona said, her tone a lot more happy. "It's Jackie! Jackie!" Fiona called, waving out the window. "Do you want to ride with us?"

"There're no more seats," Jonas observed.

"She can sit on Pete's lap," Fiona said over her shoulder.

A vision of his aunt forcing Jackie to ride in his lap to church fired Pete's limbs to motion. He flung the door open and jumped from the van. "We're on our way to church, Jackie," Pete said, noticing how beautiful she looked in a long red skirt and white fluffy sweater. "Did you need something?"

"Yes," Jackie said, her voice soft. Even at twenty paces he could tell she wasn't herself. "Can we talk, Pete?"

Chapter Seven

"Of course we can talk," Pete told Jackie. To his family Pete said, "You go on. I'll catch up." He closed the van door and crunched across the snow to stand in front of Jackie. "Are you all right?"

"Yes." She swallowed, her eyes sparkling in the sunlight that cast cold brightness over the morning. "No. Maybe I'm not totally all right."

"Come inside." Taking her by the arm, he led her indoors. She wore white mittens, a white scarf and a cream-colored coat, which set off her dark hair. But it was the look in her eyes that caught Pete's attention. Her eyes were sparkling, but it wasn't a happy sparkle. "Have you been crying?"

She didn't reply. Instead, she took several deep breaths.

She was scaring the hell out of him. Pete's heart skipped into faster beats. "Come sit down," he said, taking her by the arm and leading her into the family room of the main house. "Can I get you something? Water?"

"No. Thank you."

He waited, his breath caught in his chest. Whatever she wanted to talk about, she seemed to be hesitating. Maybe she regretted giving him the boot. Was there a chance she wanted him back? His heart soared at the thought.

If he could only be so fortunate.

"Jackie," he said, "tell me what's on your mind."

"I think I'm pregnant," she said, so softly he nearly missed what she said.

He couldn't help the grin that spread over his face. "What did you say?"

"I think I'm pregnant." And then she burst into tears.

"Oh, wow." He laughed, delighted. "This is great! Why are you crying?" Suddenly, he was bewildered. Why was she crying? Wasn't a baby a great thing? A miracle?

"Because I'm pregnant!"

"Oh, no, no, don't cry, Jackie," he said. "I'll take care of you. And the baby."

She jumped to her feet. "I don't need to be taken care of."

"Well—" He stopped, considered the mulish set to her face. "You don't want me to take care of you?"

"No."

He frowned. "But that's what men do. They take care of their women."

"I am not your woman."

"If you're having my child, Jackie, you're my woman."

"You sound like a caveman." She blew her nose into a tissue, which he thought was darling. She was so upset— and just like a woman, insisted she didn't need help when she so obviously did.

"If you don't need anything from me, why did you come here?" Pete asked, trying to reason with Jackie. Make her understand that clearly she did need him.

"Because everyone in Diablo will talk. So I just thought you should be the first to know."

Pride puffed Pete up. "We'll get married, Jackie, and no one will be the wiser nine months from now."

That brought a fresh burst of waterworks.

"We never talked about marriage before. Not really. Not seriously."

"True," he said, pulling her toward him. She allowed him to rub her back as she buried her face in his chest for a moment. She felt so good to him. He'd been dreaming of a reason to touch her again, see her again and now he'd been handed this golden opportunity. He was going to be a *father.* "Aunt Fiona will be so happy."

"What?" Jackie raised her head to look at him.

"Oh, Aunt Fiona wants us all married." Smiling, he touched his palm to her cheek. "We need to be married and have children if we want her to will us the ranch."

She blinked, her dark-brown eyes wet with tears. "What are you talking about?"

"Rancho Diablo. Aunt Fiona seems to be trying to make us believe she's on her deathbed. She's not, of course. Jonas says she's strong as a horse and will probably outlive us all. But," he said, brushing his lips against hers in a fast kiss, "now she claims she's changed her will. Whichever of us gets married and has the most children will inherit the ranch."

"So Rancho Diablo would be yours, now that we're having a baby?"

Pete shook his head. "Not all mine. My brothers and I agree that we're going to split the ranch anyway. Only one of us needs to get married to get the ranch under Fiona's rules, right? So it was going to be Sam, because he…I don't know." Pete stole another kiss. "I think Sam figured it would be easier on him to get married. He's less set in his ways."

Jackie pulled from his arms. "But now it could be you. You could make this sacrifice for your brothers."

"It's not a sacrifice, Jackie." Pete reached for her hand, drawing it to his lips. "You know how I feel about you."

She nodded. "I do. Every Saturday night, I've known exactly how you felt about me."

He shook his head. "It wasn't how I feel *just* on Saturday nights. But with your schedule at the hospital, when else could we be together?"

"I'm buying a business," she murmured. "A bridal shop."

He grinned. "That's timely. Order up a dress, sweetie. We can fly to Las Vegas this weekend."

She backed up a couple of steps. "Pete, I didn't come here to get you to marry me. I simply felt it was important that you be the first to know that we're having a baby."

"And that's great. I'm thrilled. Boy, am I thrilled." He was. He wanted to whirl Jackie around the room in his arms, laughing. He couldn't understand why she didn't seem off-the-floor happy.

"I've got to go," she told him. "Thanks for listening."

He grabbed her hand as she turned to leave. "Where are you going?"

"Home." She looked at him, her delicate dark brows high above her beautiful eyes. His heart sank as he decided she looked annoyed with him.

"And you need to catch up to your family," she said.

He was pretty certain she was giving him the royal

wave-off. "I can go to a later service. Right now, we have a million things to talk about. And, Jackie," he said, deciding to try to get a fast point in while he could, "I'd like you to start thinking of home as wherever you and I decide to live."

She shook her head, an imperceptible motion that he realized didn't bode well for him. "No, Pete. When I broke up with you, I didn't see a future for us. This doesn't change anything."

He stared at her. He couldn't swallow past the lump in his throat. Something told him to go easy, not to explode, not to lose his mind over what she was telling him. Now was not the time to push Jackie for decisions. Everything was too fresh, too raw. "All right," he said. "I guess I'll have to respect that."

She nodded. "Thank you."

When she pulled her hand from his, he didn't stop her. This time, he let her go. He listened as the front door closed, heard her boots crunching the snow as she walked to her truck.

He moved to a window to watch her. She got into her truck and he thought he saw her glance toward the house. Then she drove away.

He let out the breath he'd been holding. "Miss Jackie Samuels, you and I have a lot more talking to do," he murmured.

That little woman could run all she liked, but in the end, the only place she was going was right back into his bed—where she belonged.

Whether she believed that or not.

He was hit by a sudden urge to drive right down into Diablo and buy the tiniest pair of western boots he could find, dark-brown and masculine as heck and just right for a baby boy who would one day grow up to be a rodeo badass like all the other Callahan cowboys. "Yeehaw!" he yelled in triumph, punching the air with his fist. "I'm going to be a dad!"

JACKIE WAS DONE WITH TEARS. Done. Never crying another tear over Pete Callahan. The man was a dunce. "You do realize," she said to Darla when she met her at Diamond's Bridal so they could look over the stock, "that men are insane? They have some kind of chromosome that is unique to them that causes them not to think like rational humans?"

"Well," Darla said, "men say we're the ones who are wacky."

"Maybe." Jackie stepped inside after Darla unlocked the door. "All I know is that Pete Callahan takes the cake for crazy."

"Come look at this wedding gown." Darla held up a hanger sheathed in a white covering. "You won't believe your eyes. This one's vintage."

"Do we sell vintage in our shop?" Momentarily, Pete and his antics flew right out of Jackie's mind.

"Some ladies really like vintage, so I think we should. If you like the idea, that is. What do you think about this classic?" Darla unzipped the bag and carefully pulled out the fairy-tale creation.

"Oh," Jackie murmured, touching the tiny crystals and luminous sequins, "it's like something out of Cinderella."

"Exactly what I thought. So when Sabrina brought this dress to me—"

"Sabrina McKinley?"

"Fiona's friend." Darla nodded. "The one who's going to work for Mr. Jenkins."

Jackie blinked. "But isn't she a fortune-teller?"

"And we're nurses selling wedding and maid-of-honor gowns. Changing jobs isn't all that unusual. Some people like change. Like us."

Jackie looked at Darla. "Is she not going to do fortunes anymore?"

"I didn't ask." Darla hung the gown on a hook. Late-morning sun streamed through the window, dancing on the crystals. It seemed the wedding dress came alive with passion and wishes and dreaming.

"That's the most beautiful gown I've ever seen." Jackie's breath hung for just a second as she thought about wearing something that wonderfully lovely for Pete.

Darla zipped the gown back into its bag. "I bought it because it's totally stunning, and somebody will buy it, probably the first day our shop is open. We're in this to be profitable, and this gown is a sure sale." Darla headed to the back of the store. "And Sabrina said she was low on funds, so it seemed the right thing to do. I hope you don't mind that I bought it without consulting you. I promise never to make business decisions without you, but I couldn't resist the gown. I swear I could hear it talking to me."

"What did it say, exactly?" Jackie followed Darla after a cautious glance at the covered gown. Darla was right about the dress: it would make a woman feel like a princess on her special day. Jackie almost thought she heard a chorale of softly tinkling bells luring her back to it.

She turned off her imagination.

"It said, 'I'm perfect for your friend, Jackie,'" Darla said, stopping outside the storeroom.

"You'll wear it before I will," Jackie said, "I'm expecting a baby."

Darla turned to stare at her, then her stomach. "Sabrina was right!"

"Oh, pooh." Jackie dismissed that notion without a qualm. "You're a nurse. You know how these things work, Darla. A little nausea, some tiredness, more nausea, that's all the fortune-telling a woman needs to know she probably needs to take an in-home pregnancy test."

"Okay," Darla said, "last night you were swearing you weren't."

"I got suspicious, so I decided to take a test." Jackie sat on a stool. "I've been moody lately—"

"Just a little."

Jackie shook her head. "And so there it was. The reason for the moodiness, the desire for pickles and chocolate cake, all foretold by a little blue line on a stick."

Darla threw her arms around Jackie. "It's wonderful news!"

Jackie smiled. "I keep thinking I'll wake up and it'll be a dream, and then my toes curl and I pray it's not a dream." Jackie laughed. "I never thought I'd be a single mom, but for some reason, going into debt with this business makes me feel very optimistic about the future."

"Really? No regrets?" Darla asked. "You might prefer the steadier income of nursing."

"But not the late hours and long shifts." Jackie smiled. "Everything is happening at the right time."

"What did Pete say?"

The smile left Jackie's face. "That he's happy. He wants to get married."

Darla squealed. "You can still fit into the magic gown!"

"Now wedding gowns are magic?" Jackie laughed.

"Well, you never know." Darla flung her arms around Jackie again. "I'm going to be a godmother!"

"How did you guess?"

"Because I'd kneecap anybody else who tried to take my place." Darla squealed again. "So if Pete wants to get married—"

"No," Jackie said, the smile sliding away again, "we're not getting married."

"But if Pete wants to—"

"He really doesn't."

Darla snorted.

"He never asked me before. He was happy with our relationship just the way it was. I'm not going to drag him to the altar after I'd just broken up with him, Darla." Jackie peered into the stockroom, intrigued by all the boxes. "Let's get down to business and forget about weddings right now, okay?"

"Won't be very easy, considering where we work. But all right." Darla followed Jackie into the storeroom. "Pete's going to be a hard guy to say no to."

"Not really. If he gets married, he gets Rancho Diablo. Call me crazy, but I don't know if this marriage enthusiasm is about me or the ranch."

"He gets Rancho Diablo?" Darla asked. "All of it?"

"There's some complicated rubric of how the brothers would split it. They just need a sacrificial lamb to get married, and Fiona wants to turn over the ranch. Any of them can be the stooge, but Pete thought about me. I can't decide how I feel about being included in his caper."

"Is that what Pete said when he proposed? That this was great timing or something?"

"I can't really remember. It all sort of ran together.

But that was pretty much the gist of it. I got the feeling it was a two-birds-with-one-stone moment for him."

"That's not good," Darla said. "That sounds like a business proposition."

"That's right," Jackie said. "Just like buying this shop."

"Oh, hell. That means Judah will have to find a bride!" Darla pulled out some veils that looked like they'd seen better days. "These are some of last season's leftovers that could neither be sold nor returned. We're not going to do a whole lot of this kind of vendor business. Besides, these are not magical." She put the veils back away. "What am I going to do?"

Jackie agreed; the veils were not "magical." "We'll make better selections, although it may take us some time to develop our own vendor relationships."

"I meant about Judah."

Jackie's gaze flew to Darla's. "You're serious, aren't you? You really are crazy about him." She looked into her friend's eyes, seeing the worry there. "You're in love with him!"

Darla nodded. "Always have been."

Jackie thought for a minute. "Well, if one of them has to get married," she said thoughtfully, "it could be Judah."

"Newsflash—he's never knocked on my door."

Jackie couldn't bear the look on her friend's face, a cross between resigned and hopeless. "Why don't you ask him out?"

"No. Didn't you just say that Callahan men have a strange gene that makes them…strange? Who knows how he might take a woman making the first move?"

"It's not a first move. Judah could use a wife. Technically, it could be considered a date with his destiny."

Darla shook her head. "We focus on making you re-alize that you can't turn down a hot cowboy like Pete. Not when you're having his baby. You have to think of that, Jackie."

And then it hit her. Hard, like a snowball in the face: From now on, she was thinking for two.

JACKIE AND DARLA FINISHED going through the store's stock, examining every cabinet and drawer, checking out anything that needed to be repaired before they signed the final paperwork to take over the building and the business. "Everything feels very organized," Jackie said.

Darla nodded. "I agree."

The shop bell rang. Pete walked in, despite the Closed sign on the door, and Jackie's heart fell into her boots.

"Hello, Pete Callahan!" Darla said, cheery as all get out. "What's that you're carrying? A little friend?"

Pete set the black-and-white puppy on the counter. "Mr. Dearborn's wife, Jane, called about a litter of puppies. This is Fanny, a border collie. She's looking for a wedding shop to live in. That's what she told me, anyway."

Jackie picked up the puppy, cuddling her. "Hello, Fanny."

"I'm going to run grab a cup of coffee. Either of you want anything?" Darla asked, slipping on her down jacket.

"No, thanks," Pete said, and Jackie shook her head.

"Be back in a jiffy," Darla said.

"Pete," Jackie said when the door closed behind Darla, "what are you doing here?" She held Fanny just under her chin for support and comfort, the fat wiggly puppy body comforting. Jackie's eyes drank in the tall cowboy, even though she'd just seen him this morning.

Pete was too big, too manly, to be in a bridal shop surrounded by white gowns. The shop seemed smaller with him in it, as though the walls had shrunk. Jackie wanted to put the puppy down and reach for Pete instead, but she couldn't. She'd broken up with him. Hugging him, holding him now, wasn't fair to either of them.

"I stopped by to see your folks. They told me you were here." Dark-blue eyes stared at her, leaving so much unsaid.

Jackie hesitated, before handing the puppy back to Pete. He put the small creature inside his suede jacket, and Fanny seemed delighted to be up against his broad chest. Jackie forced her gaze back up to Pete's face. "You went to my parents' house?"

He shrugged. "I went by your house first. When you weren't there, I decided to check with your folks."

In the five years that they'd been seeing each other on Saturday nights, Jackie had never taken Pete over to her parents'. "They don't know about the baby yet."

"I figured as much. I didn't bring it up." He studied her for a moment. "Consider Fanny a bribe."

"A bribe?" Jackie looked at the brown-eyed puppy peering out over the jacket zipper. "For what?"

"Just think about making a family with me." Pete took her hand. "We need to be together."

She blinked. "Saturday-night fun doesn't translate into wedded bliss."

"I'm good with the sneak peek I got."

He grinned at her, slow and sexy and teasing, and Jackie's heart jumped. From the other side of the store, she could practically hear the magic wedding gown singing a siren's song of temptation.

But then what? What happened after the magical gown and the fairy-tale wedding? They'd never even mentioned *feelings* to each other. Never.

Jackie swallowed, telling herself to ignore the gown—and Pete.

"I brought you something else," Pete said.

He set a pair of the tiniest western boots Jackie had ever seen on the counter. Picking one up, she studied the hand-sewn leather.

"You're crazy, Pete Callahan. You don't even know if we're having a boy or a girl."

"They're unisex as far as I'm concerned."

Jackie couldn't help laughing. "I don't want these. I'll keep Fanny, though not as a bribe. Just because she's a sweetheart. I've always wanted a dog." She ran a finger along the puppy's nose, and Fanny rewarded her for the affection by trying to nibble on her finger. "I'll have to ask Darla if you can be our store pooch, Fanny."

Pete's mouth twisted in a wry grin. "Go out on a date with me, Jackie."

"No. No dating. We didn't for five years. No reason to start now."

He put a finger on her chin, pulling her close over the puppy's head, and gave her a long kiss. "There's several reasons. I'm going to marry you, Jackie Samuels. You might as well accept that."

She pulled away, wishing he'd kept kissing her instead of talking. "Pete, getting married at this time runs counter to everything I've ever believed a marriage should be about."

He took her hand, giving it a quick brush against his lips. Jackie couldn't take her eyes off his lips as they moved across her skin. "I promise to make love to you more than just on Saturday nights, Jackie, if that's what's worrying you. I promise to fit in an occasional Tuesday as well."

She turned away, not wanting to laugh. "Pete, it's not funny."

"Okay." He turned her back around. "I'm leaving now. I'm taking Fanny with me, because you're too busy for this wild girl at the moment. What time are you going to be home tonight?"

"We'll finish up around four. I should be home at five. Why?" Jackie didn't trust the gleam in Pete's eyes.

"Expect me to be waiting for you at your house. I'm going to have dinner ready for you, a fire in the fireplace and probably some romance on the side. If you're lucky."

"I'm not sleeping with you, Pete." She put a hard tone in her voice, so he would know that part of their lives was over.

"Oh, don't worry, Jackie. Like you always said, why should you buy the steer if you get the steak for free?" Pete gave her a devilish grin. "I'm all about the purchase now, so you're just going to have to do without, my sweet."

Jackie put her hands on her hips. "That's fine." *I'll try to sit on the sofa primly and act like I'm not lusting after your big gorgeous body, you ape.* "Just so we have the rules straight."

He leaned over, giving her a quick kiss before she could protest. "The rules are straight. I expect you to stick to them."

"Pete Callahan, don't try to act like I was only after your body."

"Weren't you? I could have sworn you were always more than happy to get me naked, Jackie Samuels."

She gasped, outraged at his cockiness, although he

was right. He just didn't have to rub it in, the louse. Pete laughed, turning to walk from the store. Jackie considered throwing something at him, but the only thing close enough was a veil, which wouldn't have quite the effect she wanted.

He stopped in front of the magic wedding dress, considering it through its clear plastic casing. "This would look beautiful on you," he said. "You should think about it before my son starts making you plump." He winked, knowing her blood was now on full boil, and waved Fanny's paw at her before leaving.

Jackie let out her breath, wishing she had thrown something, anything—and realizing she wished it was tonight already, when she'd be seeing Pete again.

Bad. Oh, that was a very bad sign. He was taking over her life, and she was letting him, as though they were already halfway to the altar, full speed ahead and never mind the reasons she knew better than to say yes to him.

Then her gaze lit on the tiny brown boots Pete had left on the counter. How long had she waited for Pete to show her that he cared? How many years had she hoped their relationship would turn into something?

Now it was—and it felt all wrong.

Baby boots—not booties. Boots. Already planning for a rodeo rider, a cowboy, a Callahan.

Jackie shook her head. *Forget about it, bud. I'm not raising a heartbreaker like you.*

Chapter Eight

The solution was simple. Jackie knew it as soon as she saw Judah striding across the town square. If Jackie could get Judah to ask Darla out, and things happened between them—what couldn't happen with a sexy male like Judah, and a smart woman like Darla?—then Pete would be relieved of the pressure to get married.

She'd be off the hook. All this rush-rush-hurry-hurry Pete would go away. They could relax, think about how they wanted to be parents apart from each other.

"Judah!" Jackie waved at the handsome cowboy, getting his attention before any of the females who'd suddenly appeared in the square could.

"Hi, Jackie." Judah grinned at her, walked toward her with that loose-hipped Callahan saunter. Pete walked just like that, and it never failed to make her knees weak.

"Listen, Judah." Jackie hesitated, trying to formulate a quick plan now that the object of her manipulation was in front of her. What would Fiona do? "Darla had a date tonight with a guy from out of town. She bought a new dress and everything. The loser stood her up."

Judah's gaze flashed with sympathy. "His loss."

Jackie smiled at him. "I hate for her to sit at home tonight when she was planning on going into Santa Fe."

"Does she like this guy?"

"Oh, no," Jackie said, her gaze honest and wide. "But I think he's crazy about her, and you know Darla. Never wants to hurt anyone's feelings."

"That's true," Judah murmured. "I wish I could help, but she wouldn't want to go out with me."

Jackie blinked. "Why do you think that?"

He shrugged, his grin sheepish. "Every man in this town has asked her out. She always says no. I wouldn't be any different."

Jackie didn't dare say *oh, but you would!* She wrinkled her nose, wishing she could do better at the art of chicanery, but she was no Fiona. No one was. She wasn't artful and sly, giving people that little push they needed to do whatever they really wanted to do in the first place. "That's too bad," Jackie murmured. "I was hoping you had some free time."

"Oh, I've got time. There's nothing to do around our place. We're just waiting out Sam's wedding."

Jackie stared up at Judah. "Sam's…wedding?"

"Sure." He grinned. "He's hot into planning the biggest shindig Diablo has ever seen. He'll probably be bringing a bride to you to fit for a gown." Judah winked at her. "Make it a doozy, okay?"

"A doozy?"

"Expensive. Eye-popping. One that will be talked about for days."

Suspicion flared inside her. "Judah Callahan, are you setting up your little brother?"

Judah laughed. "I'd never do that."

Only one of them had to get married. If Sam was going to do it, then Judah might stay free long enough for her to figure out how to convince him that the only reason Darla was turning down male companionship was because she was waiting for him.

Honestly. Men were blind.

"And Pete doesn't have to get married," she murmured, not realizing she'd spoken.

"Pete? Nah. He'll never marry. Unless it's you," Judah said, giving her chin a little cuff. "And a little birdie told me you weren't in the mood for marriage."

"The birdie was smart." She frowned. Why was Pete telling her he was going to marry her if Sam was going to be the fall guy for the family? "Will Sam move away after he gets married?"

"No. He'll live at Rancho Diablo, just like always."

"What about the rest of you?" Her curiosity was killing her.

"We'll look for wives."

That didn't sound good. And Judah didn't look all that unhappy about the prospect. "Why the sudden matrimonial urge infecting you men?"

Judah laughed. "Whichever one of us has the biggest family gets the ranch. The race is on for all of us."

Jackie stiffened. Pete had left out that little detail. Pete was competing with his brothers, as if he was in a rodeo, and Pete had a head start on Sam because she was already pregnant.

"That rat," she said. "That lowdown, no good rat!"

Judah grinned. "You must be talking about Pete."

"I—" She hesitated, before realization hit her. "If you're telling me this, you're not exactly keeping it a secret."

He shrugged. "No reason to. It's best to toot your own horn if you're selling something, right?"

Every female within a hundred miles was going to set her cap for a Callahan cowboy, including Pete.

It shouldn't matter. Nothing had changed between

her and Pete—no matter what that stubborn cowboy thought.

"Judah," Jackie said, inspiration hitting her in breath-taking fashion. "How would you like to come to dinner tonight?"

He raised a brow. "What's cooking?"

"Not what. Whom. Your brother," she said sweetly. "And Darla will be there." She hoped Darla didn't already have dinner plans. But having extra people around would foil Pete's plan to press her about marriage. She wanted no part of the Callahan marriage derby.

"Sure," he said, "I'd love to watch my brother slave over a stove."

"Great. See you around five."

He grinned. "Thanks."

"Not at all. It'll be fun."

Maybe it wouldn't be fun for Pete, but it was going to be fun to watch him stew. "I'm turning into Fiona," she told her friend when Darla sailed back into the bridal shop with her coffee.

"Is that a good thing?" Darla asked.

Jackie looked at the magic wedding gown, still hanging on its hook, and thought how wonderful it would look on her friend. Clearly the wrong signals were being sent between Darla and Judah, a problem easily fixed by a casual dinner among friends. "We'll find out," Jackie said. "Darla, I think I'll have a small dinner gathering tonight to celebrate our new business venture. Do you have plans?"

"I'm free," Darla said. "I'll bring dessert."

Jackie smiled. "Just bring yourself."

PETE HAD PLANS—BIG PLANS. He'd cooked up a storm, a romantic meal that would impress even the most re-

luctant of women. And he hadn't stopped there. Jackie's
sofa, the scene of so many of their wonderful nights
watching television, was sprinkled with red rose petals.
There were candles glowing on the table. And the pièce
de résistance—him. He'd found a tux and had himself
suited up like a waiter. He planned to serve her like a
princess, shower her with attention and spoiling and
everything her heart could possibly desire.

He had on his lucky boxers, too.

"Lucky, lucky." He took Fanny out of the crate he'd
put in Jackie's living room, not far from the television,
and carried the puppy outside for a fast piddle. Absolutely nothing was going to destroy his quiet evening
with Jackie. She needed to focus solely on him—the
new him.

So he wasn't particularly pleased when Judah's truck
came to a halt at the top of the driveway. Fanny gave a
tiny yap, and gamboled toward the newcomer.

"Wow," Judah said, slamming his truck door, "you
look like a dude."

Pete bristled. "I do not look like a dude. Why are you
carrying flowers?" He glared at the pink roses Judah
was waving around like he was some kind of prince.
"Why are you here?"

"Jackie invited me to dinner." Judah grinned. "A
gentleman always brings flowers. Hope you did, bro."

Pete thought about the petals he'd strewn around the
living room. After the dude comment about his tux,
Judah was really going to give him the business about
petals. He was slightly relieved when Darla pulled up
in her truck. Maybe he could get the two of them to
shove off before Jackie got home from work. He planned
on cooking for her—grilled steaks, mashed potatoes
and toasted French bread slathered in butter—then

massaging her feet. Her toes were especially sensitive, foolproof for relaxing her. Relaxation was key for getting into her bed, a place he intended them to be for the rest of their lives—no more selected evenings. Bed was the place he could help her see things his way. Pete was pretty sure he did his best communicating in bed. "Hi, Darla," Pete said, before realizing she carried some kind of pie.

Pie was good, but not today, because it might mean Darla was coming to dinner. He glanced at Judah, who was gazing at Darla, apparently too thunderstruck to speak.

Dork. Pete looked back at Darla, who was, he had to admit, a tall, hot, golden blonde who would have fitted right in someplace warmer than Diablo, someplace she could live full-time in a bikini. "Why are you bringing Jackie a pie?" he asked, hoping he'd missed some really good reason Darla would be showing up here.

"For dessert, silly," she said, handing it to him. "Jackie mentioned you Callahans love blackberry pie, and I might just tell you that these blackberries come from Jane Dearborn's specially frozen stock."

He didn't give a hoot at the moment about Jane Dearborn's coveted blackberries that she painstakingly froze every May. He was about to ask *why the hell are you handing it to me?* when three more vehicles pulled up in Jackie's drive. All his brothers hopped out, along with Judge Julie Jenkins, Fiona and Burke, and all were bearing covered casseroles or some kind of food item. If his eyes weren't deceiving him, Sabrina McKinley had also managed to snag an invite.

Everyone was here but Jackie.

"That little minx," he muttered under his breath. She'd

outfoxed him. She was intent upon keeping every wall between them she could construct.

"Hey, Pete," people said as they filed past him carrying crockery and pot holders and other contraptions used for potluck meals. "Nice monkey suit. You the waiter tonight?" was asked by more than one person. With one last glance toward the road, he went inside to find Darla.

"Where's Jackie?"

"Closing up the shop. She said she'd be here soon." Darla glanced at the rose petals strewn everywhere. "How nice of you to have a celebration for our new store, Pete."

"Celebr—" He forced a smile. "Happy to do it."

"The rose petals are a great touch."

He glanced to see if she was ribbing him. She appeared to be paying him the first sincere compliment he'd gotten beyond the monkey suit and dude comments. "Thanks." He couldn't be rude now that he was apparently hosting a reception. "I'd probably better go check the kitchen and make sure my apelike brothers aren't ransacking it."

Darla smiled, waving a wineglass at him. "Bye."

He headed into the kitchen where it looked like Aunt Fiona and Burke were managing KP, plugging in casseroles and sorting paper plates someone had thoughtfully brought. Sabrina was chatting with Julie, and his brothers looked like stuffed scarecrows incapable of conversation.

"At least *talk* to the humans with the female equipment," he muttered to the clump of men that were his brothers, although right now was an inopportune time for them to be needy. "If you're going to bag a female, you have to somehow sneak up on them."

Sam grinned. "Is that what you've done with Jackie?"

"Hell, no. I haven't had a chance to do anything yet." He took a deep breath, reminding himself that it wasn't his brothers' fault they'd wrecked his carefully laid plans for the evening. No, all the blame could be placed at Jackie's door. "Go at least send out a mating call," he advised them as he spied Jackie making her way up the sidewalk.

Before any one else could go greet her, he met her at the door. "Oh, no, you don't," he said, taking her by the arm and dragging her over to a secluded spot behind a massive trellis covered in winter-dead leaves. "You pulled a fast one on me."

"Did I?"

She looked up at him, her dark eyes innocent. He could tell she was having an inner giggle at his expense. He vowed to kiss her later until she was very sorry for trying to be such a smartypants. "Yes, you did. And I want you to know that I've got your number now, little lady. I won't be fooled so easily next time."

"Pete," Jackie said, and he raised a brow.

"Apology accepted," he said, "now shut up and kiss me."

"That's not—"

He stopped whatever she was going to say by claiming her lips. Pulling her up close, he kissed her until she was breathless, his heart hammering like a thousand anvils being beaten inside his chest.

Then he pushed her away. She stared at him, her fingertips pressed against her lips.

"Now, you go inside and make a plate for me," Pete said, "and remember, I've got my eye on you."

"Maybe that's not what I want." She raised her chin

at him, and he laughed, giving her a gentle pat on the bottom.

"Jackie, one thing I know about you is that you like me. You liked me well enough to have me on your sofa every Saturday night for the past five years. Nothing changed except you got pregnant, and now you have to somehow figure out how to get me to the altar."

He kissed her lips when they parted in outrage.

"It's okay," he said, "it might not be as hard as you think to get me there."

Then he kissed her once more for good measure, a sweeping kiss, possessing her mouth with his tongue, just to remind her how much she liked it when he carried her into her bedroom on Saturday nights.

THE NIGHT DID NOT GO as Jackie had planned, and she had no one to blame but herself. She felt like a heel for destroying Pete's dinner plans, especially after she saw all the rose petals on the floor and sofa. She'd sent a guilt-ridden glance his way, then told herself to get a spine. He'd forced her to have this dinner, and she'd warned him she didn't want to rely on her pregnancy as a reason to reel him in.

Pete was still full of typical Callahan bravado, acting as though the tux was part of the night's entertainment. Then when Fiona, fun-meister extraordinaire, pulled out Twister for "all the young folks to play," Pete had thrown himself into the game despite the tux.

But Jackie couldn't help noticing that Pete wasn't the only one bluffing a bit. Darla and Judah acted like polar opposites on a magnet; even Twister couldn't pull them near each other. They played, but it was like watching two mannequins stiffly maneuvering into positions. Sabrina and Julie and the other Callahan brothers all twisted like pretzels, quite willing to try to get into the spirit of the game, but Jackie was worn out from trying to smile.

She couldn't stop thinking about Pete's kisses, and how her body just wanted to rock into his every time he touched her. It was all she could do to slow her brain down, remind herself that there was no going back.

And then, when Fiona and Burke toasted her and Darla's new business venture, Jackie felt dishonest. These were her friends, most of them people she'd known all her life. She felt as though she was cheating them of the truth.

She felt as though she'd cheated Pete.

He followed her into the kitchen when she went to pull out some Christmas fudge to send home with everyone.

"I'm going to go," he said, and she nodded.

"Okay." But then she couldn't help being honest, at least just for the moment. "Pete?"

He turned to look at her, his dark hair falling over his blue eyes. Rarely did a man have the combination of sexy and handsome and sweet all wrapped up in one package. "I'm sorry about tonight. I meant to protect myself, and I ended up spoiling something you were trying to do for me. It was mean. And I'm sorry."

He touched her chin. "One thing you've never been is mean, Jackie Samuels. Scared, unsure and occasionally grouchy—"

She raised her brows, drawing a laugh from him.

"But you're not mean. I just rushed you. You've got a lot going on in your life right now." He dropped one hand casually to caress her still-flat stomach. "I'm the one who should apologize. But I guess I won't." He grinned at her.

"It's better if I keep you just a wee bit annoyed with me. Eventually, you'll run out of reasons to say no."

"Maybe I won't."

"Yeah. You will." He kissed her eyelids, then her lips so softly she wanted to stay near him, touch him, all night. "We'll go slow. We can start over. I don't mind convincing you that the first five years were just good friends getting together on Saturday nights. And now the fun stuff can begin."

"You're scaring me," she said, leaning her head against his chest. "I want to believe that we'd be right together forever because we always were. I just don't think we are, Pete." It was hard to say that, but it was how she felt. People who loved each other didn't get together only on Saturday nights. They shared things, their lives, their hopes and dreams.

"Just don't forget that if I marry you, I have a head start on my brothers." He gave a sly wink. "There's so many dividends to getting one of your wedding gowns on you, it's all upside for me."

She crossed her arms. "Now *you're* being mean."

He laughed, and dropped a kiss on her nose. "I'm just reading your mind, my angel cake. I leave you to your sweet dreams of what might have been tonight, and the exquisite joy I would have given you."

Jackie stared at Pete. "You think highly of yourself."

He grinned and left. She picked up a sponge, wishing she'd been holding it just a moment ago. It would have felt great to bean him with it.

Darla came into the kitchen to toss paper cups into the trash. "How did it go?"

"Insufferable," Jackie said. "The man is an ass."

Darla laughed. "And you love him madly."

Jackie didn't say anything, but in her heart, she didn't argue the point. She wished Pete would magically appear in her bed tonight, which was exactly what Pete claimed she really wanted. "I'm fighting admitting that. I may be losing."

"He seems to know you pretty well," Darla said, wrapping up the pies that had been brought. "He's got you completely flustered. Eventually, he's going to wear you down. And you'll be so happy you'll forget to say no."

Jackie thought about Fanny. Fanny could sleep with her tonight. "There's no way a baby should make two adults, who didn't have a real relationship before, have a relationship."

"I don't know. Maybe a baby is like a bandage. Patches up all the rough spots."

Jackie stared at Darla. "That doesn't sound right somehow," she said, wishing it were true.

Chapter Nine

Two weeks later, Jackie and Darla had the grand opening of their new shop. They'd decided to name it The Magic Wedding Dress, after the gown that Sabrina had asked Darla to sell for her.

"Not that we have any magic, personally," Darla had said.

"We're going to need magic to make this business venture work," Jackie replied. "Think magical. Think hard."

Owning a half store seemed magical enough to Jackie. It looked like a wedding cake, with white shutters and pink letters scrolled on the windows. She and Darla had selected cabbage-rose-flowered settees for the ladies to lounge on while brides tried on dresses. The whole effect was comfortable and bright and romantic, and Jackie loved it to bits.

Fiona brought some of her friends to the opening. Mavis Night, Corinne Abernathy and Nadine Waters surveyed the store with delight.

"Think of the things we can cook up now that we know someone in the biz," Fiona said.

"It's almost too good to be true." Corinne smiled at the young store owners. "There are a wealth of beautiful gowns in here, Jackie. You must be so tempted!" Corinne giggled, her blue eyes dancing behind her polka-dotted-rimmed glasses.

"Not really," Jackie said, which wasn't entirely true. Secretly, she'd held the "magic" wedding gown up to herself once, surveying herself in the mirror. It *was* magical. There was no label on the gown to tell where it had come from, but it had never been worn. She wondered about Sabrina—and how much she'd talked Darla into paying for the gown. She'd meant to check the business register and had forgotten in the excitement of getting everything ready for the opening. *I'll do it tonight.*

Nadine patted her arm. "I predict you'll be wearing one of these lovely creations by spring, my dear."

Jackie backed away, keeping the smile on her face. "You ladies go pick on Darla. I'm going to check the punch."

"Whew. So that's why you never wanted anyone to know you and Pete were dating," Darla said with a laugh when Jackie retreated into the stockroom. "Smart move."

"It's just going to get worse once everyone knows I'm expecting Pete's baby." Jackie sighed. "Maybe I'll ask Sabrina which way her circus went and go join them."

Darla grinned and handed her a cookie tray. "Be brave. They mean well."

Jackie carried the tray out and set it on the white-linen-covered table. About twenty ladies milled around, admiring the dresses and wedding gowns. It was all going well. Even Fanny was on her best behavior, sitting in her basket with a pink ribbon around her neck.

Then Pete walked in, and all the ladies turned to send delighted glances Jackie's way. Broad-shouldered, tall, handsome, vital—he was every woman's dream prince. *Mine, too.* But then she shook the thought aside.

"I've come to lend my support to this shindig," Pete said, making his way politely through the crowd of ladies greeting him. "I've told my brothers that they have to put in an appearance, too."

"Why?" Jackie stared up at him, her heart practically in her throat. He was so handsome. When he looked down at her, his eyes sparkling like that, it was all she could do not to throw herself into his arms. *I should. Give the crowd of busybodies what they came for.*

He tapped her on the nose. "If you want to make this place a success, you have to have bachelors to be caught."

"You're setting up your brothers." Jackie looked at Pete in surprise. "Isn't that a little devious?"

"To dangle the lure in front of the eager fish in here?" He grinned at her, leaning forward on the counter so their conversation was private. "No way. It's high time they were caught."

She shook her head. "If they ever figure out what you're up to, they'll be annoyed."

"Well, it's all for a good cause." He looked around the store. "It's weird seeing you in here instead of at the hospital. I had fantasies about your nurse's uniform, you know."

Jackie warmed all over, in spite of herself. *Don't think about fantasies,* she told herself. *Fantasies are the past.*

"But the innocent-bride fantasy works just as well." He winked at her and took the cup Darla was offering him. "Don't you think, Darla?"

"What do I think?" Darla asked.

"That nurse or bride, white is a great color for Jackie."

Darla glanced her way. Jackie could feel the blush rise in her cheeks.

"Oh," Darla said, "Jackie's playing hard to get. You'll have to romance her with something other than the fashion color wheel if you're going to drag her out of her ivory tower." She went off to greet Fiona and company with a teasing smile on her face.

"Ivory tower, huh?" Pete asked.

Jackie glared at him. "Don't you have fences to fix? Horses to train? Chores?"

He took her hand, gently brushing his lips against it. Jackie's gaze followed him, as did twenty other pairs of eyes in the store. She flushed, the heat in Pete's gaze trapping her. "I'm heading out for a week or so with Judah," he said. "When I get back, I'm coming through the window of your ivory tower. Expect it."

Jackie couldn't think of a swift reply. Pete winked at her, turned and left, sauntering through the throng of admiring females. More than one woman shot a wistful gaze after Pete's very sexy behind.

Silence descended on the store as Pete departed. Jackie tried to catch her breath, but then the five other Callahan brothers suddenly pushed through the door, to the delight of the women inside. That meant that more ladies crowded into the store from the street, all eager to be wherever good-looking bachelors were. Out of the corner of her eye, Jackie could see Darla taking orders and ringing up sales; the ladies wanted new spring things to catch a Callahan with, no doubt.

The fire marshal's going to cite us, Jackie thought. *I'm pretty sure we have too many people in here. Too many single ladies wanting a man.*

She watched the Callahan brothers seat themselves on the cabbage-rose sofas and accept tea and cookies from helpful females. They seemed to be enjoying the attention. That was the problem, Jackie thought. Callahan men loved female attention. They ate it up like peach ice cream in summer, which put her in a totally sour humor, because she knew Pete was just the same, no matter how much he tried to act as if he wasn't.

Jackie bit back a little jealousy, telling herself that it was none of her concern what any of the Callahan men did with their bachelorhoods. Then she went to help Darla, and tried not to think about Pete leaving town for a week.

She already missed him.

AFTER THE RUSH WAS OVER and most of their guests had gone—and after the rascal Callahans had finished holding court—Darla turned to Jackie. "So, partner, this may work out."

Jackie nodded. "Did you ever have any doubts?"

Darla smiled. "I did. I just didn't share them. Kind of like you not sharing how you and Pete really felt about each other. That man is crazy about you! How did you manage to keep that under your hat for so long?"

Jackie shook her head. "Pete is not crazy about me."

"Trust me, he's crazy about you."

Pete *had* seemed different. Jackie frowned. "It's the baby. He was never this way before."

Darla laughed and pulled her blond hair up into a high ponytail. "I don't think it's the baby, Jackie. Maybe he was always crazy about you, but didn't express it the way you expected him to."

"All I know," Jackie said, "is that one day I decided to change my life. I had to move on, from everything. Then you showed up with a new business, and I broke up with Pete and everything changed. I even have a dog." She picked up Fanny to take her outside. After being made the belle of the ball, Fanny was almost too excited to be excited about going out. "Of course, I love the dog. Come on, angel, you need to get out of the store for a minute."

She didn't make it to the back door before Darla called after her. "Jackie? Did you move the magic wedding dress?"

"Hang on," she told Fanny, "I promise your bathroom break is next." She went back inside the showroom. "It was on its hanger right there. Several ladies were oohing and aahing over it." Jackie frowned. "Maybe someone moved it near the big mirrors to see how it would look on them."

Half an hour—and a Fanny excursion later—Jackie shook her head at Darla. "Are you sure you didn't ring it up for someone?"

"Trust me, I would have remembered it. I wanted it for myself." Darla looked stricken. "And I'd bought it from Sabrina. So I would have been extra certain to note the sale."

No one would have stolen anything from them. At least Jackie didn't think they would. But they'd searched the store over twice. They'd checked the register tapes and the receipts—nothing. "I can't imagine," Jackie said.

Darla sat down on a cabbage-rose sofa. "It's gone. Vanished."

Jackie held Fanny in her arms, stroking her fur absentmindedly. "It'll turn up, I'm sure."

"No one in town would dare wear it. We'd recognize it at once."

"And there wasn't anyone here who wasn't from Diablo." They'd had a steady stream of well-wishers and shoppers that day, all people known to them all their lives. "Let's close the shop up and go to my place for hot cocoa. I don't want to sit home alone wondering how a magic wedding dress disappears."

"Great idea. We just need a little Kahlua for the cocoa, and I'll feel a lot better." Darla put on her blue wool winter coat and locked the front door.

Jackie opened the drawer underneath the register to get her keys and saw a plain white envelope. *Jackie* was written on it in blue ink. "What's this?" she said to Darla.

Darla looked over her shoulder. "Open it."

Inside was cash, in hundred-dollar bills and a few ones. Jackie counted it. "Exactly the price of the magic wedding dress, plus tax."

Darla took the envelope from her. "I don't recognize the writing. It's so generic it could be male or female."

Jackie shrugged. "Someone who didn't want anyone to know they'd bought it."

"And they carried it out of here while we were busy with guests."

"We can't report it as stolen," Jackie said, "but I suppose we could get the sheriff to dust the envelope for prints."

"Except you and I have both handled it." This was true.

Pete had walked out empty-handed. She remembered because she'd been staring at his backside as he walked—and watching him jealously as other women tried to catch his eye. And she didn't think it was Fiona or any of her friends. Fiona would do a lot of things, but if she was buying a wedding gown for someone, she wouldn't be quiet about it. She'd want everyone to know. Shaking her head, she added the cash to the total of the night deposit they would make on their way home.

"Well, if it was magic, we'll never know." Sabrina

followed Darla out the back. "Not that I really believe in magic anyway." She set the alarm and locked the door.

Darla shook her head. "I do. And I believed that gown was one day going to magically be mine. You could use a little magic in your life, too, you know."

It hadn't escaped Jackie that Judah had never come over to speak to Darla beyond a casual hello. Her match-making dinner the other night hadn't worked. "I'm no Fiona," Jackie said, picking up Fanny to carry her to the truck.

"No one is." Darla laughed as they walked together in the cool night air. Neither of them saw the shadows moving behind ivy trellises that framed the store, watching as they got into their trucks and drove away.

Chapter Ten

The next day, Pete decided the first thing he was going to do when he got back to Rancho Diablo was punch his brother Sam in the nose. He'd do it right now, he thought, fuming, except that Jonas was on the way and would probably take exception. Jonas and Sam might be seven years apart, but Jonas looked out for the youngest Callahan. "Just buy the damn horse and let's go," Pete groused.

"I don't know." Sam ran one hand over the ebony stallion's back. "We may not need another champion breeder."

"Why?" Pete glanced around the well-lit barn at Monterrey Five ranch, located just outside of Las Cruces. Workers milled around blanketing horses and filling water buckets. Outside, in a lighted ring, a woman was giving a teenager jumping lessons. They'd done business with Monterrey Five before, knew they were getting an honest deal. Pete didn't know what was holding up his brother, but it wasn't the horse. And if Sam wasn't going to buy the beast, Pete wanted to get on to the next stop on their list. The sooner they finished their errands, the faster he'd be back to Jackie. A week was a long time to be away from her.

"Oh, boy," Pete muttered.

Sam looked up. "What?"

"I just realized something." Realized that he'd always spent a week away from Jackie at a time, and never had he missed her this much. "I'm changing."

Sam stared at him. "Yeah, Dad. Growing up is probably normal for an expectant father."

"Not that kind of change." Pete revisited the notion of poking Sam in the nose. "Why are you being such an ass tonight?"

"I don't know. Full moon or something." Sam shook his head. "I'm not going to buy this pony."

"Pony?" Pete snorted. "He's got hooves the size of dinner plates."

Sam sighed. "I think Fiona's in trouble, Pete. And maybe the ranch."

"What ranch?" Pete glanced around him. Monterrey Five looked great to him. Well-run, busy, clean, well-stocked—the way he liked a ranch to run.

"Our ranch."

Pete looked closely at his brother. "What are you talking about?"

"Come on." Sam jerked his head, and Pete followed him from the barn. "Thanks, Pio, we'll let you know about the horse. He sure is fine."

Pio waved at them. "Thanks for swinging through. Come by on your way back if you can."

They got in Sam's truck, and Sam turned down the gravel road. "So?" Pete said.

"So Fiona's acting funny. I'm worried."

"Fiona's always acting funny. Big deal. I'd be more worried if she wasn't being lovably eccentric. Look, there's Jonas." Pete waved at his brother, who was coming up the drive. Sam stopped the truck and rolled down the window.

"Why are you leaving?" Jonas asked. "Didn't Pio have the horse on site?"

"We were just about to call you. Sam got cold feet." Pete shrugged.

Jonas glanced at Sam, who nodded confirmation. "Where are we headed now?" Jonas asked.

"You sure you want to do this?" Sam asked. "You don't have to go all the way with us."

"Yeah, I do." Jonas nodded. "I'll at least spend a day with you before I go back to Diablo."

"Let's head to the Cracker Barrel on the main road," Sam suggested. "I'm in the mood for fried chicken and mashed potatoes."

Pete waited until Sam started driving again. "Does Jonas know you're worried about Fiona and the ranch?"

"I've only told you. If Jonas knows I'm worried, he might not buy that ranch he wants. He'll want to come in and save the day at Rancho Diablo."

"Isn't that a decision you should let him make?"

"Maybe," Sam said, "which is why I'm talking to you."

"Oh." Pete felt warmed by his brother's trust. "I say tell him. What can it hurt? Six heads are better than none."

"Well, you're the most responsible one of us," Sam pointed out, and Pete frowned.

"Jonas takes that prize."

"Jonas is a doctor. That doesn't make him the most responsible or the smartest. That would be you."

Pete raised his brows. "I'm a simple ranch hand, doing what I've done all my life."

"Jonas knows a lot about medicine. You know a lot about life." Sam pointed at him. "Not that I'm saying you know a lot about women, because you don't."

"I think I know more about women than about most other stuff." Pete was pretty sure he should be taking offense. Any minute now he probably would, but the New Mexico night sky was so pretty, like black velvet, and the stars so numerous, that it was hard to get up the energy to be annoyed anymore. The desire to punch his slowpoke of a brother had left him as soon as they'd hit the road.

"Not really," Sam said. "Look how you've screwed up the whole thing with Jackie. Major fumble, bro."

The urge to poke Sam's nose returned full-force. Pete sat up. "I haven't fumbled anything."

"Are you engaged?"

"No." Pete sat up. "But I will be."

"Word around town is that Jackie took out an insurance policy."

Pete glowered. "So?"

"Life insurance."

Pete sat back, stunned. "Fiona told you that?"

"Not this time." Sam grinned. "Darla Cameron."

"I don't believe you."

"It was all accidental. I happened to ask how they'd managed to secure financing for The Magic Wedding Dress so fast, and Darla said Jackie had an almost instant approval because she had so much cash on hand for a down payment. She didn't even put up the house for collateral. Just cash. And I said that was damn brave of her in this economy, and Darla said that Jackie was a great businesswoman, and not to worry, that she was insured to the teeth in case anything happened to her."

Pete wondered why he should care about any of this. "Jackie's smart. She wouldn't conduct business without proper insurance."

"And I kidded around and said that they better not

get into any pincushion battles or anything or Jackie wouldn't have anyone to leave her estate to." Sam paused for dramatic effect. "Darla said Jackie's estate goes to her baby. She's already had it all drawn up."

"That's nice, but really none of my business." Pete warmed up just thinking about his son. He should be the one thinking of providing for his child—a thought which instantly irritated him. His baby *was* his business. He and Jackie were raising this child together, whether she liked it or not. They should make financial decisions regarding the baby's future together—*together* being the operative word. He was supposed to be the responsible Callahan, right? "We need to hurry and get this trip over with," Pete practically snarled, and Sam laughed.

"None of your business, huh?"

Pete leaned his head back and closed his eyes. Sam had no idea how close he was coming to having that nice Callahan nose totally rearranged.

THE ROADSIDE CRACKER BARREL was hopping, which was a good thing, because Pete was in the mood for company. Color. Movement. Anything to keep his mind off his brother's remarks about Fiona. Anybody with half an eye could see that there was some truth to Sam's worry about their little aunt—she *was* acting differently. Pete had noticed it when she'd arrived at the bridal shop. She wasn't her usual giggly self. Oh, she was pleasant and social and had her pod of blue-haired friends with her, but she wasn't lighthearted Fiona.

He was going to have to have a gentle aunt-and-nephew private chat with her. Pete made up his mind to do that as soon as they got home. First Fiona, then his darling turtledove. His smart, business-minded, love apple, who was busily making plans without him about her life, about their baby. It was admirable, but she was also just a wee bit too determined to be Miss Independent for his liking. At this rate, he might not ever get back in Jackie's bed.

The thought depressed him. He lost his appetite and glared at Jonas. "So what's happening with that land you want to buy east of Rancho Diablo?"

"I'm still pondering it. I may have you come out and take a look at it." Jonas slathered a roll with butter, and munched on it happily.

Pete slid a glance at Sam, who nodded at Pete. *What was that sagacious nod for? Am I supposed to do the dirty work here?* He sighed. "Jonas, Sam's worried about Fiona. Did you ever give her a subtle check-up?"

"She slapped my hand when I tried to put my stethoscope near her." Jonas looked injured. "She's never done that before. Usually she says she likes to take advantage of what she calls my expensive over-education."

Pete nodded. "But you were persistent. Not wimpy."

"No, I was wimpy." Jonas ordered a slice of pie, apparently determined to eat the contents of the restaurant on his own, Pete thought. "I bailed. With all due respect to the little aunt, I might admit."

"I guess you can't force a patient if they don't want care," Pete said.

"Yeah, that, and the fact that she has a pretty mean slap for a tiny woman." Jonas dug into his pie with gusto. "You'd be surprised."

"Okay." Pete was getting tired of his brothers' company. "Look, she said she hadn't been feeling well. Maybe we can convince her to see Doc Graybill in town."

"Tried that. No go." Sam looked at Jonas's pie with

longing. "Are you going to be a pig or are you offering a bite to your brothers?"

"Pigging out. Get your own."

Pete looked at the checkers set up on a nearby barrel where a couple of kids were playing a game. He glanced at the fire in the fireplace, noting the happy families enjoying a meal out together. Why did their family always have to have so much drama? Nothing was ever simple. He sighed, feeling the weight of his thirty-one years. "For some reason, Sam thinks the ranch might be in trouble."

"How can it be?" Jonas asked. "Even if it had a thirty-year mortgage, it's been paid off. Mom and Dad bought it right before I was born. Surely Fiona's been making payments properly, and I doubt she's taken any liens. Any work that's ever done on the ranch, we do ourselves. And we pay cash for purchases like horses and feed and equipment. We pay the taxes out of the Callahan general fund." He speared Sam with a glance. "Why would you think that?"

Sam shook his head. "Just a strange hunch I have."

"I think she's just ready to get us married off. She's going to fix our lives." Jonas nodded. "It's preoccupying her these days."

Pete picked up his tea glass and drank. He looked at the checkers set with longing, wondering for a brief second if either of his brothers would want to play. There was no time, though. Sam was right. In some dim corner of his mind, he, too, had noticed Fiona not quite being Fiona. A little more sharp, perhaps, a bit less cheerful. "Is there a reason we don't ask Fiona to have a discussion with us on the entire business side of the ranch? Not just the buy-sell side and daily operations, which we already know about, but the financial aspect?"

Sam and Jonas looked at him.

"She's never been inclined to do so before," Jonas said.

"We've never asked. Maybe she doesn't think we're interested," Pete pointed out.

"Maybe you'd like to be the one to ask her," Sam said.

"She's going to think we think she's on her deathbed," Jonas said. "I can just hear her now."

"All the more reason to know the ranch details in-depth." Pete was warming to his topic. "Have you ever thought that she's the only person, besides Burke, I guess, who knows everything? What happened to our parents? Why did they settle here? We don't know anything. I was five when Fiona and Burke came. I don't remember much." He looked inward for a moment. Hell, his first memories were of Fiona making lunch for them, taking them to church, reading to them. Most of his memories of their parents came from the photos Fiona had put in the bunkhouse on the mantel.

Sam and Jonas stared at him, their jaws slightly agape. Pete shifted in his chair. "Well, it's true," he said, feeling defensive. "She doesn't like to discuss the past. So we've never asked. We've never even pushed her about the old Navajo who shows up on the ranch once a year. Come on. She has us totally cowed."

Fiona could cow anyone. She could cow the U.S. Marines, the Pope and the Queen of England. Pete swallowed. "In fact, I think Fiona is the one thing on Earth we're all a little bit afraid of."

"And I don't know why," Sam said. "She's been a great guardian."

"But not soft," Jonas said, "she wasn't a soft guardian. Having eleven brothers made her tough as hell."

"But maybe," Pete said, "and I'm going out on a limb here, maybe it's time to get practical. If everybody's worried, and if she's starting to do things like bring in fortune-tellers, maybe it's time to tell her we have questions. She's got answers. We want them."

Jonas and Sam sat blinking at him like owls. He wished they wouldn't do that.

"Well, you're Mr. Responsibility," Sam said.

"We elect you as spokesman. We'll back you up," Jonas said.

Pete looked at the ceiling. This was partially his fault. He'd heard Fiona hiring the fortune-teller to give his brothers some oogie-boogie story to get them to the altar. He hadn't ratted her out because he'd thought it was cute of her, in a devious-little-aunty sort of way. Frankly, he'd thought it was a great joke on his brothers. And now their suspicions were aroused. "I've got enough on my plate worrying about Jackie," he said, going weasel.

His brothers glanced at each other, then back at him. In the depths of their dark-blue eyes, he saw grave disappointment. He went to defense. "Jonas, you're the oldest, damn it. You beard the lion in its sweet little flowered kitchen."

Jonas put down his fork, pushed his plate away. "She slapped my hand just for trying to listen to her chest," he reminded them. "I don't know if I'm in particularly good graces right now. She's still miffed about that."

"Then you," Pete told Sam. "You're the baby. You can get away with anything."

"I can," Sam said, "but you're the responsible one. She'll listen to you."

"You're not responsible?" Pete demanded, knowing the answer.

"I'm twenty-six. In her eyes, that's a child. Plus, I've

always followed in your footsteps. She'll know you put me up to this." Sam grinned, knowing his argument was complete baloney.

Pete stood. "I hope you're not going to make a habit of being wusses."

"We knew you'd do it," Sam said, practically crowing, "we knew we could count on you."

Jonas popped Sam on the back. Pete hesitated in the act of signing the dinner check. "We?"

"Never mind," Sam said.

Jonas nodded. "Don't mind him. Sometimes his mouth runs off without his good sense."

Pete glared at both of them, realized a family council had been held to vote him in to the position of spokesperson with Fiona. This was karma getting him. "I'll think about it," he grumbled.

"You are the most responsible," Sam said, grinning.

Pete wondered if Jackie would agree. Which made him think about how he'd rather be sleeping with her tonight than sitting here with his plotting brothers, and that made him cross all over again. "Let's get out of here," he said. "I've got much better things I could be doing."

FOUR DAYS LATER, JACKIE HAD bad news of her own.

"Why do you want me to go into Santa Fe?" she asked Dr. Graybill. "I used to work at Diablo General. The medical care here is top-notch."

Dr. Graybill put down his chart and looked at her. "I believe you are farther along in your pregnancy than you think you are, Jackie. With your history of irregular periods, you can't be sure exactly when you conceived."

"That's true. But the doctors here can handle a routine pregnancy." She was a nurse. She had extensive training and experience. Dozens of women gave birth in Diablo every year. "I'd even considered using a midwife."

Dr. Graybill shook his head. "First, I want you to make an appointment with a specialist in Santa Fe. Or someplace else. Someone who specializes in multiple births."

Jackie stared at the doctor who'd set her broken arm when she was a child, and sutured her chin when she'd fallen on it playing street basketball with her friends. His kindly eyes looked back at her sympathetically. Jackie swallowed. "Multiple? Twins?"

"I can't tell. I hear something. It's either another fetus or some type of echo. You need to see a specialist for better information. And a sonogram." He wrote the names of a few doctors on a pad and handed it to her. "These are some specialists I know. You might plan to talk to a couple of them, get a few different opinions."

Jackie shook her head. "There are no multiple births in my family. I never even thought I could get pregnant, Dr. Graybill. I've always had such irregular cycles, and—" She stopped, realizing she sounded incoherent. How could sex on Saturday nights result in twins? "I just don't see how," she said, dazed. "I'm an only child."

Dr. Graybill smiled at her. "Well, Rafe and Creed are twins. And you might ask about their family history. Twins may run generationally in the Callahan family."

Jackie got up from Dr. Graybill's desk, her stomach hollowed out from sudden fear. She wasn't prepared for two children. She didn't want to think that there might be a problem with her baby, either. "I'll make the appointment. Thank you, Dr. Graybill."

"You're welcome."

She gave him a feeble smile and went to check out. Her head was whirling. There was no way she could be having twins. Her stomach was only barely rounded. She had gained ten or so pounds. Dr. Graybill thought she was around fourteen weeks. Her last period had been in September, and this was the third week of January.

Chills swept her that had nothing to do with the gray skies and the cold wind whipping through Diablo. She walked to the bridal shop, opening the door, closing it without even seeing Fanny lolling at her feet.

"You look like you've seen a ghost," Darla said. "Come sit down. Is everything all right?"

Darla ushered her to a sofa. Jackie sank into it gratefully. "I think Dr. Graybill's getting old."

Darla laughed. "Jackie, there are a lot of elderly people in Diablo, most of them still running the pants off the younger generations. What did he say?"

"He wants me to see a specialist." She looked at Darla. "He thinks I might be having twins."

Darla laughed.

"What's so funny?" Jackie asked, not feeling like laughing at all.

"Two little Callahans? Pete's going to double his efforts to get you to the altar." Darla giggled at her own joke, hugging Jackie when she glared at her. "You wanted change," Darla reminded her.

"Yes, I wanted change." Jackie picked up Fanny, petting her, before shaking her head. "I bet Dr. Graybill is being overly cautious."

Darla grinned as she glanced out the shop window. "Prepare for more change," she said with a giggle. "Pete's on his way in right now. You can tell him the possible good news."

Jackie sank back into the sofa as her cowboy walked inside the store. "Pete," she said weakly.

"Jackie," he said, "Darla." He tipped his hat. Darla grinned at him.

"Congratulations, by the way."

"Why?" Pete looked at Darla.

"You made it back early," Darla said, smiling as she headed to the stockroom.

Pete's gaze went to Jackie. She swallowed. No one made her blood race like Pete. Darla was probably right. Pete was going to be a very arduous suitor when he learned he might possibly be a father to twins. He'd get it into his head that he was having twin boys, just like his father, and then there'd be some bragging.

I'm not telling him until I know for sure, Jackie decided. *There's no reason to get his hopes up, and he would. Darla's right. He'll crow, and he'll think he's going to win that stupid bet of Fiona's, and he'll romance me like a lovestruck cowboy.*

And it would be wonderful.

Heat hit her as she thought about how Pete could romance her. Magic hands, persuasive lips—she just couldn't handle a super-determined Pete right now. *I'm having a panic attack. I'd say yes, whatever you want, Pete, and then I'd find out Dr. Graybill's made a mistake and then I'd have Pete dishonestly. Because I was scared.*

This was not the way she wanted to get him.

It had to be about love.

"We need to talk," Pete said. "Take the rest of the day off."

Chapter Eleven

Jackie sighed. There was kind, loving, gentle Pete, and then there was demanding Pete. Stubborn was good, Jackie told herself. A bossy, chauvinistic Pete would help her keep her eyes on her goal. "No," she said. "I can't take off. I can't leave Darla."

He sat down next to her on the sofa. "Then we'll talk here."

That might be worse. Anyone could come in at any moment, making their cozy rendezvous into some romantic foregone conclusion that wedding bells would soon be ringing. Jackie edged slightly away. "We'll close the store in a couple of hours. Surely it can wait."

He pulled her to him, kissing her thoroughly, leaving her breathless and dazed. "I've been on the road with my brothers for almost five days, if you count hours around the clock. I need time with you. And if I have to have it right here on this overstuffed floral mushroom—"

"Loveseat."

"Loveseat," Pete went on, "then I don't care who in Diablo sees us."

Jackie pulled back, blinking. This was a new Pete, a Pete who wasn't content to wait seven days between visits. "Did something happen while you were gone?"

"You've been happening to me for five years." Pete

caressed her cheek with warm fingers, and Jackie felt herself melting.

She couldn't melt.

"Pete, we can talk later." She stood up, desperate to get him out of the store and away from her before she broke down and threw herself into his big, strong arms. "I'll come by your place."

He looked at her. "My place."

"Yes." Jackie smiled at him. "Something new for us."

"I don't want new. I want old." He reached out to grab her, and she sidled away just as Fiona came in the door.

"Pete!" Fiona said. "What are you doing here? I thought you were on the road with Sam and Jonas."

"I was." Pete got up and kissed his aunt on the cheek. "I cut the trip short."

"No good horses?" Fiona asked.

"A change in plans," Pete said. "Aunt Fiona, if you have time in your busy schedule, there's something I'd like to talk to you about."

"Oh." Fiona looked from Pete to Jackie, then back to Pete. Obviously not seeing whatever she was hoping to find in their expressions, she said, "I can spare some time tonight. Will it take long? Should I have Burke make dinner for us? Jackie, will you be joining us?" Her tone turned hopeful.

"No. No Burke. No Jackie. Just you and me," Pete said.

"That sounds dull as dishwater." Fiona sniffed. Then she brightened. "Jackie, I just saw Doc Graybill, and—"

"Goodbye, Fiona," Jackie said, gently easing her out the door. "It was so good to see you. I'm sorry you can't stay longer."

"But I can—" Fiona said.

"Goodbye!" Jackie said, closing the door. Dr. Graybill would never discuss her private health concerns. But he might have said something like *When will we be hearing wedding bells?* and that would be all the encouragement Fiona would need.

Jackie turned around, leaning against the door for support.

Pete stood in front of her, staring down at her with penetrating blue eyes. She hadn't heard him sneak up behind her. Her patience snapped. Opening the door, she said, "You don't want to be late for your meeting with Fiona."

Pete leaned down to kiss her lips, right there in the open doorway where anyone on the main drag of Diablo could see. "Don't forget to come by tonight," he reminded her, when he finally released her lips. "I'll be ready and waiting."

Her knees buckled. "About that—"

"Okay," he said, "I'll come to your place. And then you can tell me what you're hiding, Jackie Samuels."

Pete went off whistling, not that he felt all that light-hearted. It gave him something to do with his lips since he couldn't be kissing Jackie right now. All he wanted to do was kiss her. He'd nearly killed Sam and Jonas on the trip. He'd had a really short fuse with them, all from thinking constantly about Jackie. He wanted to be able to kiss her every hour on the hour. "This bachelor business is for the birds," he muttered, and Rafe appeared at his side.

"You're back," Rafe said. "Did Sam find what he was looking for?"

"I don't know if Sam knows what he's looking for.

What are you doing in town?" Pete glanced around for Rafe's truck.

"Buying feed. We need some storage boxes, too."

"For?"

"Fiona's taken down all the Christmas lights. She wants to put them in color-coordinated boxes this year. Red and green, so we don't have to hunt next year. It wouldn't be so bad if she didn't have a million decorations for every holiday."

Pete nodded. Ever since they'd been boys, Fiona had insisted upon lights along the fences out front, color appropriate to every holiday, including Valentine's Day. "That means she wants the red and white ones separated for Valentine's—".

"And the green and white ones for her precious St. Patrick's. All in their own special boxes. We're going to need to build another storage shed."

Pete sighed. "Isn't there enough room in the basement?"

Rafe walked with him to the truck. "That's the thing I wanted to mention to you," he said under his breath, and Pete thought *Why am I the one elected to hear everything?*

"Fiona and Burke have been doing stuff in the basement."

"There are things I do not want to hear," Pete said, getting into his truck.

Rafe got into the truck with him. Pete was glad to have a little windbreak from the cold. He'd rather head home for a cup of hot coffee, but he couldn't exactly shove Rafe out the door.

"Not that kind of stuff, dummy," Rafe said.

"Lights," Pete said. "She's having an organizational fit, right?"

"I'm not sure. Her Navajo friend was by the other night—"

"Running Bear."

"Exactly." Rafe nodded.

"So? Chief Running Bear comes every year. Like freaking Santa Claus. Except we don't put out cookies and milk for him, and toss instant oatmeal for his reindeer."

"Yeah." Rafe looked at his brother. "After his visit, Fiona and Burke started hanging out in the basement. A lot. Every time I go to find her, she's down there. She says she's cleaning and getting ready for spring canning. But the door at the top of the stairs is always locked."

She'd locked it when they were kids, too. She was afraid one of them might fall down it in their sleep. "This is nothing new. She's just being cautious."

Rafe scrubbed at his chin. "Maybe."

"And she's probably cleaning." Fiona was a bit of a pack rat. The basement had dirt flooring and shelves where Fiona stacked her canned vegetables and dishware she used only at holidays. And of course, her decorations. There was very little lighting, just an overhead fluorescent light. "It's good that she's organizing things," Pete said, not really sure if it was or not. "I need to do some organizing myself."

"She took a long-handled shovel down there the other day," Rafe said.

Oh, hell, Pete thought. *I didn't want to hear that. Nothing good can come of Fiona and shovels.*

It means something's being dug up—or buried.

PETE WASN'T REALLY SURPRISED when Fiona wasn't at the house for their meeting that evening.

"She's gone out," Burke told him. "Emergency Books 'n' Bingo meeting."

"Right, right." Pete noted Burke was dressed in his usual natty attire, but looking even more dapper than usual. "Going out yourself?"

Burke grinned. "I've been selected as guest speaker at the Books 'n' Bingo meeting."

"Really. Where's the meeting?" Pete wondered whose house they'd snared on short notice.

"Oh, you wouldn't know them." Burke jammed a tweed driving cap on his head and headed out. "Lock up when you leave!"

Pete grimaced. He knew everybody in town, unless someone had moved in yesterday, and even if they had, Aunt Fiona would have organized a welcome committee, and he'd have heard of that. So clearly it was a secret meeting.

Fiona loved secrets.

"All right," Pete muttered to himself. "Let's just have a look-see in the basement."

He grabbed the keys from Burke's special cupboard where he kept all his butlering crap—not that Burke would appreciate his things being labeled so—and fished out the long one for the basement lock. It slipped in without hesitation. "Like taking candy from a baby," Pete said, and opened the door.

He turned on the wall sconce, heading down until he could reach the switch for the overhead fluorescent. "And then there was light," Pete said, except there wasn't. Just a dim glow that streamed out from the ceiling. He peered into the dark basement, which looked the same as always to him. Dark and a little scary, and fit for spiders and other things that went bump in the night, as well as being a perfect spot for glass jars of preserves and vegetables. "I'm hungry," Pete said. "I could go for some pears right now."

He moved off the stairwell, debated going upstairs for a flashlight. Waste of time, he thought. Rafe was nutty. Nothing down here had been disturbed; he didn't need a camping torch to figure that out. There were boxes and boxes of Fiona's ornaments and lights, and rows of her carefully labeled foods—nothing more.

Pete didn't allow his gaze to travel over to the long rectangle in the dirt floor. As kids, he and his brothers had joshed each other about it being a buried coffin. They'd told ghost stories about it, daring each other to go digging. After so many ghost stories, none of them had ever wanted to be the brave one.

"It's silly," he muttered. "We're all grown men. We're not afraid of ghosts anymore."

Creed had told the best ghost stories. He could make the hair stand up on his brothers' arms. Once Creed finished his story, usually with some kind of banshee howl or other horrible story-ending device, the boys couldn't sleep for the rest of the night. Pete's eyes would close—then snap back open to peer restlessly around in the dark for signs of spirit life.

Creed had put Burke up to rigging a flying ghost in the trees once, right where the boys had spread out their camping gear. In the night, an ungodly howl had arisen, and suddenly, something white was flying over the boys, draping long fingers of soft spirit cloth over their faces as it whipped over their heads. The boys had fled into the house, screaming at the top of their lungs—except Creed, who they realized was outside rolling in the dirt, clutching his sides with laughter while enjoying them getting the bejesus scared out of them.

The hair stood up on Pete's arms at the memory. A nervous finger of fear tickled the back of his neck. He made himself glance at the seven-by-four-foot rectangle in the dirt, and cursed to himself.

It wasn't worth it. There was nothing here. Fiona hadn't been digging—there was no newly turned earth anywhere. She'd probably been digging in the garden and run downstairs with something she was canning.

His brothers were so busy worrying about Fiona that they were beginning to imagine she was off her rocker. But Fiona was just Fiona.

"It's nothing," he said. "My brothers just need to work a little harder to occupy their fertile imaginations."

He went back up the basement stairs. He could shower and get to Jackie's by seven if he hurried—time enough to drag her out to dinner. There was no reason for them to hide anymore—their secret was out. In fact, taking her to dinner might be the best way to help convince her that she needed to be thinking about their future. Jackie might not mind being a single mother, but he didn't want to be a single father.

If he was lucky, and played his cards right, perhaps he could convince her to let him into her bed tonight, too. She just needed to know how much she needed him. And their baby needed him, too.

He needed her. Pete grabbed the door handle, and pulled out to make the door swing open. The handle resisted. He tried again, applying a little more force.

It was locked.

Pete banged on the door. "Burke! I'm in here! You locked me in!"

Burke had left. But maybe he'd come back and seen the open door. Pete had left the key in the lock. "Burke!" he yelled, banging on the door. "Rafe! Creed!"

Jonas and Sam were still on a wild goose chase to find themselves horses, Pete reminded himself. Sam wasn't going to buy anything because he claimed to be worried about the ranch. And Jonas was sitting on the fence about quitting his practice in Dallas and buying the land east of here to start his own ranch. That left Judah. "Judah!" Pete hollered. "Judah, open the damn door!"

There was silence on the landing above him. Pete balanced on the narrow step, and cursed to himself. His cursing was a comforting refrain of angry words.

It kept the silent darkness away.

"I can't take it," he said, pounding on the door. He couldn't get enough leverage on the narrow step to kick it. The door opened into the basement, anyway, so kicking it wouldn't help unless he was on the other side.

He was not on the other side. He was a prisoner in Fiona's basement.

"They'll be home soon," he told his jumping heart. Sinking onto the stair, he pulled out his cell phone. He'd call Judah, tell him to come let him out.

No cell service in the basement. "Of course not," he muttered, talking to himself to keep from getting weirded out. "When I get out of here, everybody's going to do exactly what I tell them. No more fibs. No more—" He stopped as he felt a spider—or something—whisk over his arm.

Just like Creed's damn ghosts in the trees. Pete froze, his entire being tense, waiting. It was high time, he decided, to change his life. There were too many people running around like chickens with their heads cut off.

He would not join the chicken rodeo.

When I get out of here, everybody starts listening to

good ol' Pete. Instead of being Mr. Responsibility they listen to and then ignore, from now on, it's all about what I want.

And what I want is Jackie.

Chapter Twelve

When Pete didn't show up that night, Jackie refused to admit that she was disappointed. She didn't want to call his phone. He'd said they had to talk—so if he was in the mood for conversation, he'd show up.

She told herself she was glad for the reprieve.

She missed the heck out of Pete, the old Pete. *I miss us the way we were,* she thought, but then she knew she didn't. That was why she'd wanted to change her life. She'd needed to move forward. Pete was not forward.

Still, she missed the easy companionship they'd shared once a week. "I'm in trouble," she muttered to Fanny. "I can't live with him, and I can't live without him."

It was too crazy to contemplate. Jackie sat on her sofa and snuggled the puppy, who was putting on weight almost as fast as she was. "You were some gift, you know?" she told Fanny. "I did not need a puppy and two babies."

The doctor had to be wrong. His hearing was probably a little compromised at his stage in life. She had a very small house. There was room for one child, but not two, not really.

She heard the doorbell, and went to find Darla on the porch. "I'm glad you're here. I needed company."

"I need a favor," Darla said. "Is Pete here?" She glanced around.

"No. He never came by." Jackie shrugged, trying to act as if it were unimportant.

"Never called?"

Jackie shook her head.

Darla sat on the sofa, putting a leg underneath her and reaching for Fanny. Jackie handed her the puppy and sat down, too. "That's not like that eager-beaver cowboy."

"Probably had to do something at the ranch. They're a little shorthanded with Sam being gone." Jackie tried to sound complacent about Pete's absence. "And since I'm avoiding telling him the truth until I get the test results, that's fine with me." It really wasn't. She missed him now. But it was for the best, until she was more settled. "I don't know where I'd put two babies."

Darla eyed her stomach. "I don't, either."

Jackie sighed. "So what did you need Pete for?"

"Oh." Darla sat up. "I want his opinion on a new car."

"What's wrong with your truck?"

"I like my truck. But I'd been thinking about getting something newer, and Sabrina wants to buy it." Darla beamed. "Pete would probably have some good ideas, or know of someone who has something they want to part with."

"When did you see Sabrina?"

"She came in after you left. She says she's enjoying working for Mr. Jenkins. And she likes living in Diablo. So she thought she might get a new truck. Hers is awfully dilapidated, you know. So then I said I might be looking to sell." Darla grinned. "Your theory of change is rubbing off on me."

"My theory hasn't been going too well, if you haven't

noticed." Jackie shook her head. "I'll call Pete and see if he's still coming by." She was glad to have the excuse to call him. He was usually punctual to a fault. His cell phone kicked instantly over into voice mail. "It's not like him to be this late." Or late at all.

"Mr. Reliable," Darla said. "Let's go check on him."

"Check on him?" Jackie sat back on the sofa. "Why would we check on a grown man who lives on a ranch with a ton of other people?"

"Fiona and Burke are at Books 'n' Bingo. Jonas and Sam are out of town. Creed is in Diablo picking up supplies."

"That leaves Judah." Jackie frowned. Judah was the wild Callahan, the complete opposite of Pete. He rode bulls for a living, so that was likely the bad-boy draw for sweet, business-minded Darla. "You just want an excuse to see Judah."

Darla stood and kissed Fanny's small black nose. "Is that a bad thing?"

Jackie took Fanny and put her into the crate. "I'm not sure this is a prudent plan."

"We have no plan," Darla said.

"That's true," Jackie said, and went to get her coat.

PETE FIGURED HE'D BEEN in the basement around an hour, and he wasn't happy about it. For one thing, Jackie would probably be steamed that he hadn't shown up. For another, he hated sitting and twiddling his thumbs. He was a man of action, a man who didn't like sitting in a dark basement with no idea of when he might be sprung from exile. "This is why I never break the law," he said out loud. "I'd be no good with confinement."

Besides which, Sheriff Cartwright's tiny jail wasn't exactly home sweet home.

Then he heard it: The welcome sound of soft voices. "Hey!" he yelled, banging on the door. "Someone open the door!"

He heard footsteps, and the door sprang open. Jackie stared down at him, and a more beautiful sight he'd never seen.

"Pete? What are you doing down there?" Jackie asked, but he wasn't going to bother with explanations until he snagged a kiss from those sweet lips. He laid one on her until she was breathless, and then he was breathless, and then he realized he couldn't stand not sleeping with her another week, not even another day.

"You weren't down there a month, Pete," Darla said, and Pete broke away when he realized they had an audience.

"Sorry," he said, "it felt like a month." He grinned at Jackie, feeling better already. "To what do I owe the pleasure of your company? Which I'm very grateful for, by the way."

"What were you doing down there?" Jackie asked again.

Pete shrugged. "I went to check on something, and then someone locked the door, not realizing I was in the basement." He repressed a shudder, forced a grin and reached for Jackie again. "I made some personal decisions while I had nothing to do but think in the dark, and some of those decisions include you, my turtledove."

Jackie looked at him. "The door wasn't locked."

"It was." He nodded. "I couldn't budge it."

"She just opened the door when she heard you hollering like a madman," Darla said. "I watched her."

Pete stepped back, glanced at the doorjamb. "It was locked."

Jackie and Darla didn't say anything. Pete realized

they didn't believe him. But it had been. He'd tugged on that doorknob with all his might, and the knob hadn't so much as offered to turn. "It must be getting old," Pete said. "I'll buy a new one and replace it."

"We came by because Darla wants to talk to you," Jackie said. Pete felt warmed and comforted just standing in her gaze. "About cars, if you're sufficiently recovered from your misadventures."

He looked at her, hearing a note of teasing in her voice. "You don't believe me. You think I'm a wuss who can't open a door in a house I've lived in all my life."

Jackie giggled. "It's a good thing Darla insisted on coming by to find you."

"Good to know someone cares," he said. "You have no idea how big the spiders are down there. I need some fresh air. Car talk over a veggie pizza, ladies?"

They headed toward the front door. Pete glanced over at the basement door, unable to get over the feeling that someone had pulled a not very funny, Callahan-style prank on him.

THEY ATE PIZZA, then Darla left, since she'd gotten "all the car advice she could stand." Pete had offered to take Jackie home, and Jackie had accepted. "This is the first time we've been out in public, thanks to Darla," Jackie said.

"I was just thinking the same thing. From now on, there's no need to hide from the lovable local busybodies." Pete grinned at her, so handsome that Jackie felt her breath catch. "I made some personal vows while I was locked in the basement that I think you should know about."

"Pete." Jackie smiled at him. "You panicked."

"I may panic at times," Pete said loftily, "but doors are not that hard for me to open. I promise I'm capable."

"I know. But everyone's known for a long time that you...you know."

"That was a rumor Jonas floated. I am not claustrophobic." Pete tried to look offended. "You know my brothers lie like rugs. Fibbing is a way of life for them."

Jackie laughed. "You are all capable of some pretty tall tales."

He put his hands over hers after the pizza had been cleared away. "Jackie, I'm not that claustrophobic."

"Just a little scared of the dark?"

"Not if you're there with me." He lifted her hand to kiss. "I can be quite brave."

She pulled her hand away, giving him a mock stern gaze. "Jonas said you were always afraid of small dark spaces, things that went bump in the night, and that at your family campouts they could always count on getting a rise out of you."

Pete shook his head. "If you'd been a favorite target of your siblings, you'd have always been looking over your shoulder, too."

"And commitment scares you. Anything that feels like it might tie you to something." Jackie tapped a finger against his hand. "Confess."

He grinned. "Try me, lady."

She sniffed. "So are you going to share some of these thoughts you had during your dark sojourn in the basement?"

"Yes." He nodded, his gaze suddenly sage. "We're getting married next week."

She blinked. "No, we're not." She had a doctor's appointment in Santa Fe next week. There were questions she wanted answered first.

"We are. Jackie, everyone always wants my advice but no one wants to take it. I'm asking you to marry me next week. We'll fly to Las Vegas. Or we'll stay here and have it done. I don't care which. But my son is going to be born with my name on his basket."

"Basket?"

"Whatever they put babies in now." Pete looked at her. "If you want me to get down on my knees right here in the—"

"No," Jackie said quickly. "Let's go discuss this rationally. This is the darkness and the small confined spaces talking, Pete. In the morning, it will wear off."

He helped her from the booth. "Nurse, your professional opinion is appreciated but not needed. I'm not having a panic attack. I was having a panic attack when I was trapped in the basement, but now I'm calm as a sleeping baby."

"A sleeping baby?"

"Well, whatever else you can think of that's calm. And I'll be calm next week when we say I do."

She sighed. It was going to be a long night. "I don't want to get married." She tried to sound bold and very determined, even if all she wanted was back in his arms.

Pete helped her into his truck. "Jackie, marrying you is my top priority."

"Priorities are great, but—"

"Glad to hear it," Pete said, "Saturday night, then."

Chapter Thirteen

"Pete, come in," Jackie said, "just for a few minutes."

They'd been silent on the ten-minute drive from the restaurant. Jackie let Fanny out of her crate, and the puppy went running to Pete with tiny yips. Pete picked her up, nestling her for a minute against his chest, before saying, "I'll take her out."

Jackie went with him. The moon was round in the January night sky, and the thousands of stars shone like diamonds. Crisp air blew gently across them as they watched Fanny explore her backyard.

Before she knew it, Pete had taken her in his arms, kissing her as though she was a delicate doll he didn't want to break. She could feel him taking his time with her, trying to show her that everything would be all right.

"Pete," she said, pulling away a little from him, however much she knew she belonged in his arms, "Dr. Graybill wants me to have some additional tests next week in Santa Fe. I really don't want to think about planning a wedding, too."

Concern flashed into Pete's eyes. "I'll take you to Santa Fe."

"No, no." Jackie shook her head. "I know you're shorthanded at the ranch. And I don't need anyone to go with me."

"I'm going," he said, and she realized tonight was Stubborn Pete night.

In a way, it felt good to know he was so concerned.

"So, what does the doctor say?" Pete asked.

They sat on the porch while Fanny explored.

"He wants me to be checked for the possibility of a multiple pregnancy." A small reassuring smile lifted her lips. "It's a wild goose chase. I think I'm having a normal, single pregnancy. But he wants me to have it checked, so I've made an appointment."

"Multiple?" Pete stared at her. "Like…twins?"

"Yes." She nodded.

"Wow," Pete said. "We have twins in our family. It's a possibility." He thought about it for a moment. "Rafe and Creed drove me nuts. They drove everyone nuts."

Jackie laughed. "I know. Pete, don't worry."

"I'm not," Pete said, "I'm trying not to yell with joy."

"Really?" Jackie looked at him shyly. "I was so scared to tell you. I thought it might be too much for you."

"You're weird," Pete said. "Every man dreams of twins."

She laughed. "Now you're overdoing it."

"Well, okay, I don't know about most men, but I wouldn't mind twins at all. Two boys," he mused. "Jackie, you're an amazing woman. All those years you thought you couldn't get pregnant, and you might just have hit the jackpot." He tickled her ribs, taking some playful nips along her neck. "I changed my mind. I don't want to get married next Saturday. I want to wait until you're big and round as a prize-winning pumpkin at the

State Fair, so everyone can see what a good shot I am. I'll grin while you waddle down the aisle."

"Pete!" Jackie pushed him away, though not very enthusiastically.

He pulled her into his lap. "My proficient little nurse," he said, "who would have ever thought your eggs would like my—"

"Pete Callahan," Jackie said, making her voice stern. "Bragging is not a good trait in a man."

"I don't care," Pete said, "my brothers are going to explode with envy. I can't wait."

"No, they're not," Jackie said, "they've set you up."

He looked at her. "What do you mean?"

She wished he hadn't brought up the bet. "Have you noticed any of them charging out to get a date?"

He frowned. "No."

"I could barely get Judah into the same room with Darla. I think they're happy to let you get tied down."

"They're slow starters," Pete said, but his frown didn't go away.

"Would you be so happy if you weren't currently beating your brothers in the race for the ranch?" Jackie asked.

"Yes, because the whole thing is dumb." Pete ran a hand over her cheek, cupping her face to his. "Fiona has a lot of harebrained ideas, and this is one of them. You have all the babies you want, my little lamb chop. We'll live right here in your house, and stack their cradles up like condominiums."

Jackie smiled. "At least I don't have a basement for you to lock yourself in," she said, and he snagged a fast kiss in retribution.

"I'm only interested in your sofa. Let's go inside so I can reacquaint myself with it."

PETE SLEPT ON THE SOFA, with Jackie's head on his shoulder. He hadn't meant to fall asleep, but she was so soft and round, and it felt like home, and the next thing he knew his watch was chiming its usual four-thirty wake-up call. He carried Jackie into her bedroom and set her on her pretty white bed, and when Fanny begged to get up, he put the puppy up beside her. Fanny snuggled into the blankets next to Jackie's stomach, and Pete wished he could do some snuggling of his own.

Instead he stole a tiny kiss from Jackie, who barely stirred. His angel needed her beauty rest, since she'd only had about four hours of sleep. His sons needed their rest, too. He grinned.

Life was just getting better all the time.

He let himself out and headed to the ranch. He'd forgotten all about the chat he was supposed to have with Fiona until he found her in the kitchen. She looked as though she'd been sitting up all night waiting for him, something she hadn't done since they were teenagers. No matter how late they'd tried to sneak in, she'd been perched at the kitchen table like an energetic owl.

"Good morning," he said, kissing her cheek. "Can't sleep or up early?"

"Early!" Fiona snorted. "You haven't gotten up earlier than me a day in your life, Pete Callahan. And Burke's out starting your chores. He didn't think you'd make it back."

Pete got himself a cup of coffee. "When have I ever slid on the chores?"

She frowned at him. "You've been off in your own world lately."

"I have? Who missed our meeting last night?"

"I forgot about the Books 'n' Bingo meeting when I said that." Fiona gave him a sour look. "Anyway,

I figured whatever you wanted to talk about could wait."

"You just skipped out, Aunt," Pete said cheerfully. "I'll catch you when I get back from the morning rounds." *And then tonight, I may head over to Jackie's and let her seduce me. I'm pretty sure I won't say no.*

Fiona looked at him. "What time did you leave last night?"

"Around nine. Why?" He paused at the door, his coffee mug in his hand.

She jerked her head toward the back of the house. "Were you in the basement?"

"I got locked in down there, and Jackie and Darla let me out."

She sniffed. "And my jars?"

Pete went down the hall. The door leading to the basement was kicked off its hinges, hanging against the wall at a jagged angle. "Holy crap," Pete said as he walked down the stairs. He flipped on the overhead light, his eyes huge. Every single one of Fiona's precious jars of vegetables and preserves had been smashed. "What the hell happened?" Pete said, eyeing the pile of shattered glass on the floor.

"We thought you might know," Fiona said from behind him.

He stared, his mind refusing to accept what he saw. The mess was terrible, the smell of ruined vegetables and fruit overwhelming. "I am so sorry. All your hard work, Aunt Fiona."

"Never mind that. Who was in the house last night?"

"Just me and Jackie and Darla. Everything was just fine last night." Except it hadn't been. He wondered again about the lock. He went back up the steps, staring at the door carefully. There were no scratches on the lock. Someone had simply kicked in the door. "I locked it. I put the keys in Burke's cabinet. What time did you and Burke get back?" His blood chilled as he thought about Burke and Fiona coming in while someone was ransacking the basement.

"Around midnight." Fiona's shoulders slumped. "This isn't good."

"Have you called the sheriff?" Pete followed her into the kitchen.

"No," Fiona said on a sigh. "I can't."

He looked at her. "It's time we talked, Fiona," Pete said, and his little aunt just nodded, looking defeated.

"But I don't want your brothers to know anything," Fiona said. "It's imperative that you keep this conversation a secret, Pete."

"Secrets are bad, Aunt Fiona."

"Secrets are *necessary*," she shot back. "Promise me."

He sighed. If Jackie was right and his brothers had set him up to be the marriage fall guy, then they were keeping secrets of their own. All his resolutions were going out the window in record time. "Fine," he said, "I think."

They sat down at the kitchen table. Pete waited for his aunt to speak. It was clear she was choosing her words carefully, not certain where to begin, so he reached over and took her hands in his.

"Bode Jenkins wants the ranch," she said, taking him by surprise.

Pete stared at her. "So? People in Hell want ice water, as you've always said."

"I can't stop him from getting it," Fiona said, and Pete realized his aunt was worried and frightened and everything a woman her age shouldn't be. He saw the suffering on her face, and knew it had been in her heart for a long time.

"I'm sorry, Aunt Fiona," Pete said. "You should have told me sooner. I had no idea you were carrying around this burden."

She shook her head. "I didn't know how. You boys... you were entrusted to me, as was this ranch. Burke and I have done our best, but—" She let out a shattering sigh. "Bode's just plain outsmarted me."

"Nah." Pete squeezed her fingers. "No one outsmarts my aunt."

She looked at him, her usually bright eyes filled with tears he knew she wouldn't shed. "Do you want me to go over there and kick his ass?" he asked, meaning it to be playful, just to put a smile on his aunt's face, but she shook her head so quickly he knew she was afraid he'd do just that.

"I couldn't tell you boys because I was afraid of what would happen. All six of you have heads like bags of microwave popcorn. I never know when the hot air might suddenly explode."

Pete shook his head. "Why don't you start at the beginning?"

Fiona nodded. "It's been happening for years, a sort of slow creep I was pretty proud I was fighting off. Cattle would disappear. I figured he was trying to run us out of business so we'd have to sell. That was easily solved, I just put up extra fence and kept the cattle elsewhere."

"Of course it's difficult to keep your eyes on five thousand acres and six nephews," Pete said, thinking about what his aunt had gone through.

"Well, we were up to the task, but Bode didn't make our lives any easier." Fiona pulled her hands back from his and put them in her lap. "As long as nothing happened to you boys, I didn't care. I wasn't worried when the acreage down near the ravine caught on fire. Didn't get overly excited when he sent a couple of brawny men over to put an offer on the ranch." She sniffed. "I sent them packing in a hurry."

Pete reminded himself that he'd just solemnly promised his aunt he wouldn't go thrash the daylights out of Bode Jenkins. He could feel the blood boiling between his ears, though, and told himself to remain calm for his aunt's sake. "I'm sure they never bargained on you," he told Fiona. "I wish you'd let us help you, though."

"You were younger then. And I was supposed to be your guardian. Frankly, I've got enough Irish in me not to be afraid of a little battle between neighbors," she said with a rueful smile. "Tell you the truth, I always thought Bode was dumber than a rock. But I didn't foresee his daughter, Julie, whom I'd held on my knees when she was a baby, growing up to be his ace in the hole." Fiona shook her head.

"How?" Pete asked, trying to imagine sweet Julie being much of a threat to anyone. She could be a rascal, and certainly raised hell on his brothers when she deemed it necessary—and he'd always admired her for it—but Julie was a lady.

"Next thing I knew, about five years ago, the discussion of eminent domain came up. That alarmed me, as you might imagine. Suddenly, the state was talking about needing our land for a highway. Burke and I fought it, of course. They weren't willing to pay a whole lot for the property, and I felt there were better avenues to consider. So we suggested alternative routes to the state, and to our surprise, they agreed with us. I thought it was over. I should have been suspicious then." Fiona took a deep breath. "We had the property paid for, the house paid off, it was all Callahan. And then Judge Julie was appointed to the state federal bench. Julie does whatever Bode wants her to do, as I suppose any good daughter would. So, we were told we had a year to relocate. It's been six months now. We've run out of appeals."

"What does this have to do with Julie?"

"Bode's buying the land. There's nothing we can do about that. He has a deal with the land commissioner—thanks to Julie—to take over the property. It's no secret that Bode may be an unpleasant person, but the old miser's a savvy investor and has been sitting on his wealth for years. And he has lots of friends in high places."

"You have lots of friends," Pete murmured, thinking of his social little aunt.

"Not political friends. My friends play bingo, read books, raise their kids. I was never politically minded. You'd be surprised what money can buy."

No, I wouldn't. Pete shook his head. "So what was the hurry for all of us to get married and have children for a ranch we were never going to get?"

"Oh," Fiona said, "I just wanted you boys to get down off your slow-poke butts and give me some babies. While we still have the ranch, while we can still have weddings here if you want to, why not? Before everyone finds out how low the Callahans are falling."

He regarded his small, determined aunt with some puzzlement. "You wanted us to find brides who would think that they were marrying into the Callahan family name, but would later find out we weren't what they thought we were?"

Fiona sniffed. "Marriage is full of surprises. Anyway, it wouldn't matter if you boys picked women who loved you."

He hesitated. Jackie wouldn't care if the Callahans

still owned the biggest and best ranch around or not. *But I might*. The truth was, everything he had, everything he thought he was, was tied up in this land, a place where his sons would never run and play the way he and his brothers had. His heart felt like it was breaking. "I guess you considered selling off part of the ranch."

She nodded. "For about half a second. No longer than that. Bode would just get injunctions. I couldn't bear to part with anything my brother and his wife had built, anyway. But I do despise Bode Jenkins, who is a thief if there ever was one."

It was really hard not to get up and go kick Bode's ass. Pete couldn't stand to see the worry etched on Fiona's face. She'd carried this burden so long by herself. Pete got up. "Don't worry, Aunt Fiona," he said. "Everything is going to be fine."

"Except the basement door got kicked in," she said, and he stopped.

"Do you think Bode did that?"

She shrugged. "Nothing was taken."

"We don't keep cash in the house." That was all kept in a locked safe, whose whereabouts only the eight of them knew. They'd been vigilant about people breaking in to their home, knowing it would be a temptation.

"I don't know for sure," Fiona said, "but I think Bode has wanted this house for so long it's just about made him crazy."

"This is simply solved. I'll just go ask Sabrina if Bode left the house last night."

"Oh, no," Fiona said faintly, "you can't ask Sabrina that."

"Why?" Pete sat back down, realizing he was about to hear more.

"Because I hired Sabrina to be a fortune-teller and tell you boys that you had to get married."

"I know." He nodded. "I heard the whole scheme."

She raised her brows. "I know that. I could see your shadow and your big ears practically pressed flat against the tent wall."

He looked at her, finally grinning. "Not much gets by you."

She nodded. "But what you didn't know is that I also hired Sabrina's sister, Seton, who is a private investigator, to dig up dirt on Bode."

Pete's jaw dropped. "Aunt Fiona!"

She jutted out her chin. "I finally decided two could play dirty, and that all was going to be fair in love and war. And I love nothing like I love my boys."

He was stunned. "We love you, too, redoubtable aunt...but is that why Sabrina McKinley is working as his caregiver? She's really a mole?"

"Sabrina is neither a fortune-teller nor your usual caregiver. She is an investigative reporter. She was doing a piece on animal cruelty, which is how she wound up at the circus. I met Sabrina and Seton through my friends. They are nieces of Corinne Abernathy."

Pete closed his eyes. "Does the sun ever rise without your cagey little brain working on a new scheme?"

"Nope," Fiona said happily. "I feel so much better now that I've told you all this, Pete. You have no idea how cleansing that was!"

His head felt as though it was about to explode. "So you want to ruin Bode?"

"I want," Fiona said with deadly purpose, "to make sure he never gets my brother's property."

"Maybe we could just talk to Julie?"

"Bah," Fiona said. "Bode's her father. Who would you

believe in? Who would you want to make happy? Your father or your neighbor? The people who live on five thousand acres of prime land while you've grown up on a postage stamp of canyon in a tiny wooden foreman's house next door?" Fiona waved a hand at Pete. "He's got her convinced he's at death's door so she'll live there taking care of him, waiting on him hand and foot. She'll never marry because of that old fool. She's got her job, which makes him happy because of the political clout, and he's got her. Life is happy for Bode Jenkins, the miserable rat."

Bode wasn't the only one capable of playing the feeble card. Pete remembered Fiona working that angle a bit with Jonas. Or maybe she hadn't been. Pete scrubbed at his morning stubble. "You still don't think that telling the others would—"

"No." She shook her head. "You're the only one who's rational enough not to go do something stupid. You're the only one responsible enough to realize that there's more than one way to skin a cat without getting fur in your mouth. I can count on you, Pete."

He sighed and reached over to pet his aunt's delicate hands. "Yes, you can, Aunt Fiona. Everything will be all right."

He just wasn't sure how.

Chapter Fourteen

Pete did the lion's share of the chores he needed to do, realizing a thousand questions were still left unanswered. If anything, his aunt had given him more things to ponder. Fiona never told a whole tale—there was always one more curve just ahead of the brothers' slower brains. But one thing he did know for certain: He had to talk to Jackie.

At noon, he found her at the wedding shop. "Can I buy you lunch?"

"Oh, Pete," Jackie said, her hair delightfully mussed as she moved dresses around the shop, "today is rearranging day. Darla and I have planned to organize the merchandise by classification." She smiled at him. "But thanks for the invite."

He looked at her, wanting nothing more than to carry her off on his white steed and make love to her for about a week. He was certain he'd feel much better after he did.

Unfortunately, he had no white steed—only black-as-night Bleu—and Jackie wasn't the kind of girl who'd put up with heroic nonsense like a man just riding off with her. She'd tell him he was a chauvinistic ass and probably lame him. "Jackie, I need to talk to you."

She looked at him over the top of a wedding gown. "About?"

He brightened. "That one suits you."

"What one? Oh." Jackie hung the dress on the rack. "Don't get any ideas, Pete. I have no intention of walking down the aisle."

That was the trouble. She had no intentions. He had a short deadline. Fiona was right—he'd love to get married at the ranch, while they still had it. "Could you rethink that? I was hoping we could stick to the I-do-next-week plan."

"No. I have to get my appointment in Santa Fe taken care of. I can't think past that." She hauled another dress over to a different stand.

"Those look heavy." He frowned. "I thought wedding dresses would be airy and light. Maybe you shouldn't be carrying them."

"Pete!" Jackie laughed. "You're going to get in trouble if you try to supervise my pregnancy."

"Well." He shifted, not exactly certain how to get Jackie to succumb to his wishes. "I'm coming with you to the appointment. Wild horses couldn't keep me away."

"I might let you. Maybe." She shot him a glance. "If you don't drive me nuts between now and Monday."

"Monday?" He perked up. "So soon?"

"Dr. Graybill called their office. So they fit me in." She slid some plastic off some dresses to examine them. Pete watched her morosely. How could she stand to look at wedding gowns every day and not want one for herself?

"Is there something wrong with me?"

She glanced at him. "Other than you can't get yourself

out of a basement that isn't locked, no. You seem all right to me."

He decided not to tell her that the basement had been trashed sometime in the night. Fiona hadn't really wanted their personal family business broadcast. He frowned, realizing Fiona had never mentioned who she thought might have done it. Bode wouldn't stoop that low if he thought he was already getting their ranch. Fiona had no enemies to speak of. He and his brothers might have enemies, but none of them would stoop to being so wienie as to destroy preserves. Someone had gotten into the house and locked him in—he was sure of it. Then when he'd left, they'd gone through the basement.

Someone was looking for something. And someone was watching their comings and goings. He and his brothers weren't around much. It was just Fiona and Burke, two stalwart, older folks on a big ranch where no one would hear them if they needed help.

Maybe he was overthinking it. Yet it did occur to him that the only new people in town were Sabrina and her yet-to-be-seen sister, Seton. He didn't think he completely approved of his aunt's plan to hire spies, but Fiona had never asked for his approval.

"Pete?" Jackie said, and he snapped his gaze to her face. She was lovely. Pregnancy was making her blossom. He'd always thought the myth about a pregnant woman glowing was something women said to make themselves seem desirable, but Jackie was more beautiful than ever. He wanted her, right now.

He had to put those thoughts away for the moment or he was going to ravish her in the store. "Yes?"

"Are you all right? I was teasing about the basement."

"Yeah, I know." He moved his hat back on his head. "Jackie, let me ask you a theoretical."

"Okay."

She wasn't really paying attention to him. Her gaze had gone to the window. He glanced, too, seeing nothing unusual on the Diablo town streets. "Say I had been locked into the basement."

She smiled. "All right, let's suppose you had been."

"And then you let me out, which I should reward you for later."

Jackie looked at him. "Is that part of the question?"

"No." He shook his head. "If someone went into the basement not too long after I'd been locked in, and made a big mess—although I'm not saying that happened— would you suppose the two events were related?"

Jackie shrugged. "If things had happened in that way, and no one in your house was responsible for the mess, one might think that the house was searched while you were locked in. And then when you were let out of the basement, it was searched. That's what you're trying to tell me, isn't it? Someone's been in your house?"

He held up a hand. "It was just a theoretical."

"Has someone been in your house?" Jackie's eyes were huge. "What would they be looking for?"

"No, no," Pete said, wondering why he hadn't thought about someone being in the house while he was conveniently locked away. "Don't go jumping to any ideas."

"I'm not. You are. You just wanted me to say it out loud to give your brain permission to think it. It was there all along."

"No, I wasn't."

"You set me up to give you the answer you wanted. You know, you're more like Fiona than you think you are."

She went back to rearranging dresses, which he hated to see. He was pretty certain heavy lifting couldn't be healthy for his little wife in her condition. He wondered how Jackie would take to him mentioning that she should probably quit working until the stork arrived.

He frowned. "I'd feel better if you were staying with me."

She stared at him. "Why would I want to be in a house where there's a random thief wandering around? Isn't that what you're trying to tell me?"

He shook his head. "I said nothing of the sort, and Fiona will kill me if you share that gossip with anyone. I just want you near me. My motives are pure, I swear."

"I can't tell if you're being romantic or a pain in the ass."

"Both?"

She smiled. "Tell you what. You go away now, and I'll make you a salad for dinner."

"Salad?"

"I'm watching my weight. Too much weight gain isn't supposed to be good for the baby. And for some reason, the weight seems to be packing on pretty quickly now."

"I can handle a salad," he said, thinking she looked sexy as hell to him, "but I think my sons need more sustenance than rabbit food. How about if I bring them a steak?"

She waved him out of the store.

"Rare, medium or well done?" he called as she pushed him onto the sidewalk.

"Goodbye, Pete," Jackie said, but he swiped a fast kiss and went whistling down the sidewalk.

Jackie went back into the store, trying to remember

what she'd been doing before Pete had come in, nearly undoing her resolve where he was concerned.

"I've said it before and I'll say it again. That man is crazy about you," Darla said. "How can you keep such a sweetheart at arm's length?"

Jackie shook her head. "Pete just likes the chase. He'll get tired soon enough."

Darla didn't look convinced. "Maybe you underestimate him. He seems like he's made up his mind. Once you told him he was going to be a dad, he's made a point to see you every day he can."

Jackie thought about that, the surprise of it catching her off guard. "You're right."

"Yes. And you're the happiest I've ever seen you."

Darla was right about that, too. She sighed. "Life is tricky right now. Pete and I were always about the cozy, comfortable sex. I don't know what's going on, but I know sex would not be cozy and comfortable right now. My waistline is expanding at warp speed." She shook her head. "I do not feel sexy at all."

"Give him a chance. He may like caftan-wearing, big-bellied ladies." Darla grinned. "You don't know until you strip, girlfriend."

"Eek." Jackie supposed she could keep the lights off, but she was pretty certain in the history of women trying to do the same, that plan had often backfired. "I miss the days of candlelight, don't you?"

Darla laughed. "Go for it. Buy a bunch of candles. And let that gorgeous hunk decide whether he can handle you big and babylicious or not. I'm thinking he's not going to be all that focused on anything but naked you."

Chills ran all over Jackie at the thought of Pete being in bed with her again. She missed making love with him.

She missed his deep voice whispering husky naughty things to her. Missed his arms wrapped around her and going to sleep knowing he was beside her until the dawn.

"I'm going out for a minute," Jackie said.

"Go get him, Tiger!"

Jackie hurried after Pete. "Pete!"

He was walking down the sidewalk, big-shouldered, tall and lean, and it didn't escape Jackie that about ten women were casting their eyes at him, saying hello, trying their best to get his attention. *Mine,* she thought, and then stopped, horrified. Her pregnancy wasn't easily hidden now—in fact, it was pretty obvious despite the empire-style, long-sleeved, fashionable dress she wore— and she was running after Pete.

To hell with it. "Pete!"

He turned, grinning at her, his brows raised as she made it to him slightly out of breath. "You shouldn't be running like that, angel cake. You might pull a hamstring."

She wanted to punch him. He looked so smug, so proud of himself, and he was even more handsome, if that was possible.

"Did I forget something in the store?" he asked, clearly enjoying his big moment of being the pursued.

"No," Jackie said, "and you're not making this easy on me." Out of the corner of her eyes, she could feel the faces peering out of windows watching her and Pete.

"I'm enjoying your eagerness, my pet."

"I simply wanted to tell you," Jackie said, her teeth starting to grit, "that maybe I'd feel better if you were staying with me."

"Oh, you're worried about me." He swept her into his arms, leaving no one in any doubt about the status of their relationship. If he'd shouted *I'm the father* to the rooftops, he couldn't have been more clear. Part of Jackie rebelled at his chauvinism, but a bigger part of her snuggled against his chest. She felt the smile stretch on her face.

"Yes. I'm worried about you, you ass. You shouldn't be in a house where there are creepies hanging around."

"I can't leave Burke and Fiona."

Clearly he wanted her to beg. "Leave them a shotgun."

"Jackie!" He turned her face up so he could look down into her eyes. "Do I actually hear welcome and anticipation and—"

She pulled away. "Don't overdo it, Pete Callahan."

He laughed, sweeping a finger down her nose. "I'll be there for dinner, pumpkin pie. Don't you miss me too much between now and then. And I'll take very good care of you."

She couldn't miss his meaning. Nor could about twenty people milling around nearby, acting as though they weren't listening to every word. Jackie's face flamed. She was going to flee, until she caught sight of some of the town's more eligible females eyeing her with envy, so she rose on tiptoe and kissed him right on the mouth.

"If I'd only known how much you like an audience, my sweet, I would have insisted on our relationship being out in broad daylight a long time ago." Pete laughed, saluted her with a devilish wink in his eyes, and walked off.

Jackie stared after him, her blood pounding in her ears. Okay, she looked like she was pursuing him. She was pregnant, she was running after Pete and she didn't care who saw.

She'd caught him. And she couldn't wait until to-night.

She went to buy some candles. And then, for good measure, she bought a lacy pink and white nightie, not caring at all that the whole town would know how crazy she was about Peter Dade Callahan.

JACKIE FELT PRETTY BRAVE about her plan until Pete strolled into her house that night. He looked tall and long and lean, and raffish with his rumpled dark hair, a devil-may-care bachelor if there ever was one. And she felt frumpy.

"I brought steaks," Pete said, laying a grocery sack on the table. "But I vote we have dessert first."

"Wait, Pete." Jackie tried to avoid his hands, but he was too fast for her. She didn't have on the sexy nightie, which she was hoping would deflect the eye and make him concentrate on anything but her big tummy and boobs that would no longer fit into her bra without spill-ing out the top. The candles weren't even lit yet, and she needed the cover of candlelight.

"I'm done waiting." He carried her into her bedroom, kicking the door shut behind them. He laid Jackie on the bed, his mouth claiming hers, but Jackie gave him a halfhearted push. "Pete, let me get you dinner first. You must be starved."

"You guess correctly." He buried his face in her neck, nibbling kisses as he unbuttoned her dress. "There.is far too much material here. You're wrapped up like a mummy. I know it's thirty-two degrees outside, but too much dress conceals the good stuff." He slipped it off her shoulders. "Jackie," he said, grinning at her, "you've been keeping things from me."

She laughed as he undid her bra. "Pete," she said,

trying to hold on to her bra. He was having none of that.

"Goodness," he said, his tone admiring, "come to daddy." And then his mouth was on her breasts, and Jackie forgot to be embarrassed about the size of them. Her dress seemed to melt off her, and Jackie clutched Pete to her, pulling off his shirt, shoving his jeans down, craving his warmth.

"Hi, boys," he said to her stomach, kissing the whole rounded size of it, and the last worry Jackie had floated away. "If they're napping," he told Jackie, "I'm about to wake them up."

"Pete!" Jackie tried not to laugh, but his playful spirit washed away her insecurities. All she wanted was him. "We don't know that we're having twins."

"It's either that, sweetie, or a linebacker. Or you swallowed several pumpkins." He kissed her stomach again. "I'm going to have to turn you around so I don't hurt you."

"Why?" Jackie put her arms around his neck, pulling him down to her so she could kiss him. "You're not going to hurt me."

"I don't want to jostle them."

"Let's find out if they like being jostled."

"I don't know," Pete said, "you were hiding a lot under those baggy clothes, Jackie. I don't want to press my boys flat as pancakes."

"Either you get inside me right now," Jackie said, "or there will be hell to pay."

"Yes, ma'am," he said, sliding between her legs. And then he was inside her, and Jackie gasped as he kissed her hard, driving her mad with feeling him again.

He only hesitated once. "Am I hurting anything?"

"For the love of Mike," Jackie said, practically growling, wanting him never to stop doing what he was doing to her.

"Pete," he said, "I prefer for the love of Pete." And then he found the sweet spot, and Jackie forgot to be mad. Closing her eyes, she let the sweet waves of pleasure claim her, going boneless and mindless and utterly content to be in Pete's strong arms. She felt him stiffen, heard him cry out, and holding him close to her, finally allowed the pleasure she'd held back to wash over her like rain.

"Pete," she murmured, "I missed you."

"Say it," he said, rising above her, still inside her, "go ahead and say you can't live without me."

She slapped his rump smartly. "I can't live without you."

"Good," he said, groaning, "because I'm pretty certain I can't live without you, either. I don't get munchies like my brothers. I get the Jackies, and I just have to have you."

She giggled as he buried his face in her neck, nibbling on her. It was so hard to be mad at Pete that it wasn't worth the effort.

I just love him too much. And I don't know how to fix that.

A HALF HOUR LATER, Pete realized he'd fallen asleep. "Oh, hell," he said, pushing himself up on an elbow so he could look down into Jackie's face, "I think I short-circuited." He kissed her to make up for the lack of pillow talk.

Jackie giggled. "You have been acting strange lately."

"It's sympathetic pregnancy pangs. They're blowing all my fuses. Are you hungry?" God, he was a louse.

He shouldn't have fallen asleep like that. All his good intentions flew out of his brain when he got in Jackie's bed. He didn't think he needed food, even. He could probably just live on sex with Jackie for the rest of his life.

"Starving."

"I'll get the steaks on." He hopped up, grabbing for his jeans.

"Pete?"

He turned to look at Jackie. "Uh-huh?"

"About that other position you mentioned we might try."

Had he hurt her? He felt his heart rate jump. He'd never touch her again—at least not until his little guys were born—if he'd caused her the slightest bit of pain. "What about it?"

She crooked her finger at him.

"Oh, boy," Pete said, throwing his jeans back on the floor.

Chapter Fifteen

Forty minutes later, Pete knew he was wearing a very self-satisfied smirk. "We've got to stop meeting like this."

Jackie giggled. "Naked?"

"Once a month. Let's go back to our old routine, at least." Pete wondered how he could convince her that they needed to meet like this every night—married. "We have to buy a bigger house."

"*We* have to buy a bigger house?"

"Mmm." He kissed down her neck to her collarbone, lingering at the spectacular view. Pregnancy certainly brought out the best in his turtledove. "Now that the whole town knows we've been living in sin, we might as well go ahead and do it."

"The whole town doesn't know it."

He grinned, running a palm over her tummy. "Even if you hadn't branded me in the middle of the street today, my love, I think they suspected. It's time you make an honest man of me."

Jackie tried to roll out of her bed, but he caught her and brought her back, sneaking a hand between her thighs. He heard her breath catch, and grinned. "Say yes."

"To what?"

She sounded like she might be relaxing to the point of mindless, so he decided to press his advantage. "To the bigger house, for starters."

"Pete," she said, moving away from his hand and pushing him down on the bed so that she straddled him. He grinned at her serious expression. She was going to try to read him the riot act, and it was so cute when she tried to do it naked. It took all the seriousness right out of it. He could feel her warmth and wetness on his stomach, and if she only but knew it, his soldier was standing at attention right behind her. Waiting patiently for her to finish.

"If I'm having one baby, and that's what I think, there is no need for me to move. This house is plenty big enough. And I never said I'd share a house with you."

"This is a two-bedroom, one-bath house. We need a bigger house, Jackie, one that's far out in the country. You yell loudly when you're aroused." He kissed her fingertips, nibbling at them and then up her wrist. "You came so loudly Fanny ran under the bed. She may never come back out."

Jackie took her hand from him and crossed her arms, which did nothing but stiffen parts of him that were already at attention. He put his hands behind his head, enjoying the delicious sight of rounded, nude Jackie.

"I did no such thing. I made barely any noise."

"My sweet." He gave her a mock-ashamed look. "You're so loud that the chandelier is still swinging in the living room. I think the house moved on its foundation."

He lifted her hips and sat her on himself, grinning at her gasp. He reached up to tweak her nipples as she moved on him, enjoying watching her find the spots that pleasured her. But then she leaned over, and her breasts fell into his face so he could lick and suck on her nipples, and all Pete could think of was how much he loved Jackie Samuels, no matter how hard she tried to run away from him.

He was fast. He'd catch her yet.

"I ADVISE COMPLETE BED REST," Dr. Snead said on Monday, turning to glance at Jackie and Pete.

Pete didn't think Jackie on complete bed rest sounded all that bad. Bed was exactly where he wanted her. But Jackie looked concerned, so Pete said, "Is there a problem with the pregnancy?"

Pete had driven Jackie to Santa Fe Monday morning after the longest weekend of lovemaking he'd ever enjoyed. He thought he just about had her under his spell. Things were looking positive, anyway, since she used to shoo him off on Sundays and not open the door again until the next Saturday.

He looked at the screen the doctor had returned his attention to, and held Jackie's hand. She was squeezing him until his fingers were numb, and he squeezed back, letting her know that everything was going to be fine.

"No problem," Dr. Snead said. "It's just that the three babies are taking up a lot of space inside Jackie. And she's already mentioned having spasms. We need to keep the babies in as long as we possibly can."

The room swam around Pete. Now he was clutching Jackie's hand. The nurse pushed a stool underneath him. *"Three?"*

Dr. Snead nodded. "Three heartbeats. Three well-established babies. It's hard to make out the different bodies because they seem to be tangled up in there. But here's an arm."

Pete brightened. "Can you tell the sex?"

"Girls," Doctor Snead said. "It'll be clearer later on, but unless someone's got a thumb down there I can't see, you're having three girls, Jackie."

Jackie's face was ashen. Pete rubbed her hand in his. "I always knew you were an efficient woman, Jackie. We're going to have an entire family."

"I never even thought I could get pregnant," Jackie said, sounding close to tears. But she was smiling, and Pete realized she was pretty much in shock. "But I can't be on bed rest," she told Doctor Snead. "I have a shop to run."

"Get a recliner and a portable phone," the doctor said. "I'll send a nurse out once a week to check on you. And I suggest you, Mr. Callahan, learn how to cook and clean."

Pete grinned at Jackie, his face creased with mischievous laughter. "I can cook and clean, Doctor."

"And I'm afraid no marital relations," Dr. Snead said.

Pete patted Jackie's hand. "There goes your plan of driving me mad with sex, sweetheart. You'll have to do without the pleasure of me until after the children are born."

Jackie looked as though she had plenty to say but was refraining until the doctor and nurse had left the room. Pete was so happy he couldn't stand it.

He was having three little girls. All those squiggles and lines he couldn't make sense of on the screen were three little Callahan cowgirls.

After having nothing but brothers, he was looking forward to being the only man in the house.

"Jackie," Pete said, "it'll be hard on me to wait on you

hand and foot, but it's a sacrifice I'm willing to make for the cause."

She looked as though she was about to kill him as he helped her up from the table. "What cause is that?"

"You, darling," he said. "You're my new cause in life."

"Great," Jackie said. "I'll only be half insane by this time next month. By the time the babies are born, I'll be stark raving mad."

"I've got to buy a baby name book. And a house. And baby furniture. Have you even been thinking about all this, Jackie Samuels, or has your mind only been on your new business?" Pete gave her a light pat on the rump as she bent over to slip her shoes on.

"Ugh. The next several months stretch before me endlessly." Jackie let Pete give her his arm.

"Just because you can't have sex with me," he said. "Good thing you had a lot of me this weekend."

Jackie sighed and Pete grinned. "We have to get married. We don't have a second to wait. You're not going to want to get married in a recliner, Jackie. Let's let the romance of Santa Fe lure us in to just doing it. Spontaneously."

"No." She shook her head. "Pete, I can't."

"We'll redo the vows later, if you want, after the babies are born and you've got your figure back. That's what you're worried about, isn't it? Your sexy little body fitting into a wedding gown?"

"No," she said, and he could practically hear her teeth grinding. "I just found out I'm having triplets. And I'm in love with a numbskull. That's what is worrying me." She sailed off toward the truck, and Pete followed, happier than he'd ever been in his life.

She'd said she *loved* him. Maybe that had just slipped

out from between her pretty little tightly clenched teeth, but he'd heard her. And he wasn't going to let her forget it, either.

Whistling, he followed her, feeling like a king. It was a beautiful day in Santa Fe, and he was going to be a dad—he *was* a dad—and he had a woman who loved him. All was well until he realized Jackie was raining tears like a leaky faucet.

"What is it? Are you in pain?" He leaned across the seat to look into her face.

She shook her face and blew her nose. "I wanted change. Have I ever gotten change."

"Yes, we have. Isn't change awesome?" He wanted her to cease the waterworks, though. He didn't want his little girls getting scared by all the noise their mother was making. "Change is good, right?"

"Change is great, but too much change is scaring me."

He pondered that. "Will it help if I tell you I have a surprise for you?"

She looked up at him through beautiful, watery brown eyes. His love had such limpid pools of suspicion beaming at him that all he could do was smile at her. "You look like I'm about to give you a vacuum cleaner."

"Not if you want to keep your handsome face on your block-shaped head." She sniffed.

He laughed. "Here." Reaching into the backseat of the double cab, he handed her a bag from her own wedding shop. "Be very careful how you open it, my love. My heart is in that bag."

She stared at him, more cautious than ever, and slowly pulled his gift from the bag.

"The magic wedding dress," she said, her voice awed, and Pete grinned.

"Darla said it was your dream come true. So I sneaked off with it." Pete kissed Jackie, and swept her hair back from her chin so he could see her face. He hoped to see a smile.

Instead, Jackie cried harder.

"Oh, crap," Pete said, "I knew I didn't believe in magic."

"No," Jackie said, trying not to cry, "it's sweet. You're sweet. It is my dream come true. I'm just not sure I'll ever fit into it now." Tears ran freely down her cheeks. Pete dug into the glove box for tissues. "I hate being all hormonal and emotional, especially when you're being so romantic and princely."

"You might fit into it if we hurry," Pete said, trying to tease her but really meaning it. "There's a chance you'll only grow another inch by the time we make it to a drive-through wedding chapel."

Jackie looked at him. "You're serious."

"Yes." He nodded. "Is there a better time than the present? I'm wearing my best jeans. You've got a dress. My chariot can take us there." He pounded on the dashboard. "It'll be as romantic as running off to Hawaii."

"It won't."

"I think it will be. And Callahan is a sweet last name. You might as well give in, Jackie. Remember when you told me there was no need to buy the steer if you could get the steak for free?"

"Yes," Jackie said, blowing her nose, "but now I'm not going to be getting any steak, according to the doctor."

"All the more reason to go ahead and reserve the steer for later." He kissed her cheek, and then her lips. "You can't resist me, Jackie. And those little girls are going to want to know they're fully claimed Callahan."

"I don't know, Pete. There's an awful lot to marriage besides having kids. My parents nearly got divorced when my dad went through malepause. It's bad when the parents aren't entirely suited to each other. The kids suffer." She looked at him. "Marriage is a very serious thing. You can't approach it like a rodeo, all just ride and hang on."

"Sure, that's exactly what it is. You can hang on to me for dear life." He snapped his fingers. "I knew I was forgetting something. I forgot to ask your father for permission to marry you."

He looked so upset that Jackie smiled. "You can ask him later, when we say our vows at your ranch. I always thought that if we did get married, I would love to do it at your family's ranch."

"Oh." Pete looked out the window for a second. "I don't know. Ranch weddings are kind of overdone. Eloping sounds a whole lot more spontaneous and romantic. Don't you think?" He looked at her eagerly.

She sighed. "I give in."

"Whee-hoo!" Pete yelled, punching the air with his fist. "I knew you couldn't wait to be my bride, Jackie, though you played hard to get. Awfully hard to get. *Pfew.*" He didn't want to think about that anymore. She'd agreed, and that was all that mattered. He pulled out his phone. "Now," he said, punching some buttons, "let's see how far we have to drive to get someone to marry us on the spot. I hope you have the money for this. It's bound to be expensive."

"Pete," Jackie said, laughing.

"Well, I'm not cheap. And there's still the matter of your house. If you're going to be on bed rest, I'll have to pick out the new house. Well, what do you know?" he said with satisfaction, "we can get married right here in Santa Fe. Actually, we could get married back in Diablo, but why wait? There's no blood test, you just need your license, social security number and twenty-five bucks. Do you have twenty-five bucks to buy me a marriage license?" He glanced over at her. "No? Lucky for you, I brought some spare change just in case."

"You planned this," Jackie said, and he grinned.

"Come on," Pete said. "Let's find a willing justice."

"Hang on a sec," Jackie said, "you should know I have no intention of moving."

"You just sit over there and imagine three girls fighting over one bathroom, and us waiting our turns, while I find the justice of the peace. I talked to one this morning who thought she had plenty of room in her schedule."

"Is this your version of sweeping me off my feet?"

Pete grinned. "Consider this my first act of sweeping, just like the doctor suggested."

"I don't think that's what he had in mind when he said you'd have to cook and clean."

"That's okay," Pete said, "you just visualize yourself into that so-called magic wedding gown, and let me take care of everything."

THE WEDDING DRESS fitted like, well, magic. Jackie looked at herself in the mirror, admiring the tiny crystal beads and sequins delicately placed on the white satin. It was the most lovely gown she'd ever seen. She *did* feel magical. Pete had overthought the situation as usual, slipping a pair of Cinderella-awesome shoes into the bag he'd "just happened to pick up" along with a darling bouquet of white roses he grabbed at a florist's. Jackie felt like a princess, and the glow in Pete's eyes told her she looked like one, too.

They stood in front of the justice, and Pete's voice didn't even shake when he said "I do." Jackie's knees were knocking together, but Pete was steady as a rock, his big hand holding hers. He kissed her before, during and after the ceremony, and the justice later said she'd never seen a man so eager to get his ring on.

The ring Pete surprised her with brought tears to Jackie's eyes. It was platinum, with two oval diamonds on it. "I'll get you another diamond to match, now that we know we're having three little girlies," he told her, and all Jackie could do was smile at Pete like she'd never smiled in her life.

He insisted on carrying her over the threshold of the courthouse. Jackie let him because he was so excited about it.

"Aren't you disappointed about not having a boy? You already bought boots."

"I'll take them back for some ladylike pink ropers." Pete shrugged, and she thought maybe he wasn't too terribly upset not to be getting at least one boy, since boys were all he'd talked about from the moment he'd learned he was going to be a dad. "We'll have boys next time," Pete said.

Jackie groaned. "You're still working on the bet."

"Nope," he said, "that was one of Fiona's scams." Pete looked at her strangely. "Did I forget to tell you?"

Her heart sank. "Tell me what?"

"Oh." Pete laughed, sounding a bit embarrassed. "Keep this under your hat, but apparently we've lost the ranch."

Jackie blinked, unable to comprehend what Pete was telling her. He couldn't be so blithe about something so huge. "Pete, what are you talking about?"

He sighed. "This is probably something I should have brought up before now. I got so carried away with the babies, and planning a wedding—"

"Pete. What happened?" Nervous tremors began tickling Jackie.

"I don't know exactly. I just know that getting us all married with families was a scheme on Fiona's part because the ranch is gone. History." He looked at her. "I'm sorry, Jackie. I should have told you before—"

"How can it be gone? As in, she sold it?"

"No." He shrugged. "Some convoluted problem involving Bode Jenkins. He convinced some higher-ups to declare our land for a highway. Fiona persuaded the state that a better route could be found, and thought she'd warded off Bode's land grab. By then, the state had already determined that it should be bought by them, and the final result is that it will end up in Bode's hands. Kind of like when a certain big executive decided he wanted the city to build a big football stadium in Texas, and influenced the state that the people living nearby should have to sell and move. The state may have utilized right of eminent domain to make the people move, but everyone knows who really owns the property." Pete shrugged again. "Fiona says she feels responsible, but all I can see that she did wrong is that she should have come to us, not that I know what we could have done to change the outcome."

"That's terrible! I am so sorry, Pete." Jackie couldn't imagine anyone taking her house and her little half acre. She'd paid for it with her own hard-earned cash and smarts, and she was pretty certain she'd have to be dragged off her property before anybody took it from her. "Where will the Callahans go now?"

"Fiona didn't say expressly, but I have a hunch that she's counting on Jonas to buy acreage east of here. He's wanting a spread, and we could move operations there. She sort of hinted around about it, although she didn't mention it to him. I'm the only Callahan she's told, and she doesn't want the others to know right now." He sighed. "But I should have told you, Jackie."

"Yes, you should have," she murmured. "I'm so sorry, Pete. I didn't know the Callahans were losing their livelihood."

"We're not," he said, then he frowned. "Well, I guess we are. I never thought of it that way." He brightened. "Let's go back to being happily married. I got a great girl, and you got a perfect guy." He carried her to his truck, and Jackie waited for the inevitable comment she knew was coming.

Pete didn't disappoint her.

"Good thing we got married today," he said, pretending to huff as he set her down. "I won't be able to carry you in a few days, my sweet."

"Not so perfect, after all," Jackie said, but Pete just smiled.

"Let's go put you in bed," he said. "I'm kind of looking forward to a captive audience."

Jackie shook her head at Pete and stared out the window as they drove away from the justice's. She couldn't help feeling some of the day's brightness steal away from her. Maybe she was still in shock over having triplets. Certainly she'd been so stunned that she'd willingly gotten married. Jackie gazed down at her lovely gown, and her beautiful ring and then glanced over at her new husband—a man who had somehow forgotten to tell her a huge new development in his life. She'd been worried that he was marrying her because of the bet between the brothers—now she wondered what else Pete was keeping from her.

He hadn't forgotten to tell her. Somehow she knew he hadn't wanted her to know.

Chapter Sixteen

Three months later, Jackie marveled at the amount of change that had taken over her life, her body and her husband.

"Pete won't leave me for more than an hour," Jackie complained to Darla, "and even then, he wants Fiona to be here to keep an eye on me." She held up a baby bootie she was knitting, a pink, not-ready-for-prime-time first attempt. "Fiona is teaching me to knit, but she says I'm pulling the yarn too tightly. She says I'm tense." Jackie put the bootie down and looked at Darla's sympathetic face. "I'm not complaining. It's just it's a beautiful day outside, and I want to be anywhere but in this recliner."

Pete had installed a leather recliner in the house, her "princess chair" he called it. She didn't feel like a princess. "I underestimated my husband's enthusiasm for keeping me in a prone position."

Darla handed her the week's sales numbers. "That will make you feel better."

Jackie cast her gaze over the numbers, glad to be talking business instead of baby for a moment. "Why are the sales up so much?"

"It's spring. When a young man's fancy turns to thoughts of love?"

Jackie wrinkled her nose. Pete hadn't mentioned anything lately about love. He had been asking her lots of questions, most of them had to do with how she felt—if she had any aches or pains, could she feel the babies kicking, did she want him to make a run for ice cream. "I want to give you the magic wedding dress to sell."

Darla handed her a glass of water and sat down cross-legged on the sofa nearest her. Fanny begged to sit in Darla's lap, and Darla scooped her up. "I know you're not allowed on the furniture," she told Fanny, "so be still for Aunt Darla and don't do anything that gets us both in trouble." She looked back at Jackie. "We can sell the magic wedding dress in a flash. But won't Pete be upset if you don't keep it? Aren't you supposed to redo vows again later?"

Jackie shook her head. "I don't need to redo anything. The first time was fine."

"You said you were in shock and can't remember much except Pete kissing you practically the entire ceremony." Darla giggled. "I would have liked to see that. Anyway, you promised I'd be your maid of honor."

"Did I?" Jackie wrinkled her brows. "I'm pretty sure once was enough for me. Why don't you wear the dress next?"

"Not me." Darla sighed. "I have no one who wants to kiss me breathless at an altar."

Jackie thought Judah was crazy if he couldn't see that Darla was the greatest girl in Diablo. Perfect for him, if he could only pull his head out—

"Anyway," Darla said, interrupting Jackie's not-so-nice thoughts, "I still think Pete would want you to be sentimental about the gown since he went out of his way to get it for you."

"He has a romantic side I never expected," Jackie

admitted. "But Sabrina told me that the gown isn't to be kept. The magic has to move on."

Darla petted Fanny, her fingers kneading the border collie's back and stomach. Fanny lay stretched out across Darla, sucking up all the attention she could. "Do you think Sabrina really believes all that airy-fairy stuff she spouts?"

"Does it matter? I wouldn't want to be responsible for clogging up the magic or whatever."

"Have you told Pete?"

"Pete doesn't believe in magic," Jackie said. "He'd scoff at the idea."

"I meant, have you told Pete you're going to get rid of the dress?"

"No." Jackie shifted in the chair. "There are only so many hours in a day."

Darla laughed. "All of which you spend flat on your back, usually getting your feet rubbed or your belly oiled by your prince of a husband."

"It's not that big of a deal." Jackie didn't want to discuss the dress with Pete. "Will you take it to the dry cleaners for me?"

Darla hesitated. "I'll be happy to. Why are you in such a hurry to get rid of it?"

"I told you," Jackie said, "Sabrina told me the dress's magic is in the giving."

"I don't know," Darla said. "This feels like making stock investments based on fortune cookies or something."

"It's probably a pregnancy thing. But I want to do what Sabrina says."

"Fine by me. But what if someone had bought it that wanted to keep it?"

"I guess the magic would have just stayed wrapped up

with it in the bag." Jackie couldn't explain it—she knew she'd sound too fanciful—but she *had* felt magical when she'd worn the dress. There had never been a second of doubt that when Pete gave it to her, it was a fairy-tale moment. "Why are people so silly about these things? I wouldn't expect Pete to keep the pair of jeans he was wearing when we got married."

Darla got up and rummaged around in Jackie's cabinet for a bottle of wine. "Can I get you a wineglass of organic apple juice?"

Jackie would have liked the wine. But that was several months away. "Yes, thank you. And don't change the subject."

"I'm not changing the subject." Darla handed her a glass of juice. "Maybe I will take the gown for myself, since you seem sure it really is magic. I could use a Cinderella affair in my life."

"Very selfish of you to hoard magic," Jackie said, nodding, "I approve."

Darla grinned. "It's worth a shot, isn't it?"

Jackie nodded, and sipped her juice. "We could give it a year."

"A year. I don't know, Jackie. I want Judah to fall in love with me, not some creep."

Jackie smiled, thinking about Pete and getting warm all over. "I'm sleeping every night with a big hunky cowboy now. It's worth a shot."

Darla sighed. "With my luck, all I'll catch will be geeks who live with their mothers and whose only social interaction is playing games on the internet."

"Think positive," Jackie said. "A few months ago, I was still working at the hospital and wondering if Pete and I had a future." Which seemed strange now, because she couldn't imagine not getting her hands on him every night. His protective streak got on her nerves, but that was all about the babies. Once she was out of this chair, he'd go back to being normal.

Maybe she didn't want normal with Pete.

"One year," Darla said. "That would take a lot of positive thinking. And a haircut. Maybe some clothes. A trip to Victoria's Secret." She handed Fanny to Jackie. "So, where's the dress?"

PETE WALKED IN five minutes after Darla left. He glanced around. "Where's Darla?"

"She had a few things to do." Jackie smiled up at her big cowboy. "How's the ranch?"

Pete ignored her question. "She's supposed to stay here until I get back."

Jackie frowned. "I have a phone, Pete. I don't need babysitting."

"It's not babysitting." Pete put Fanny outside. "I want someone with you at all times."

Jackie's frown deepened. "That isn't going to always be possible. Anyway, I'm fine."

"I know you are." Pete's face was slightly ashen. "I just want someone with you. Or I will be here."

There were times when he wasn't quite the prince he aspired to be. Jackie sighed. "Come over here and kiss me, you big ape, or I'll send you out for ice cream at midnight."

He kissed her, and magic that had nothing to do with a wedding dress stole over Jackie. She looked up at Pete, her gaze longing. "When I get out of this chair, you better be ready to be an eager husband."

Pete kissed her again, stealing her breath with his attention to detail. Her entire body heated up in places that remembered how good he felt.

"Oh, boy," Pete said, pulling away from her reluctantly. "I think I'll go shower."

Jackie smiled. "A shower wouldn't be too taxing on me, I'm sure. And there are things I can do for you—"

"No." Pete backed away from her chair. "The visiting nurse says you're going to have some type of IV if you keep getting those cramps. Something to help keep the babies inside."

All the warmth left Jackie. It was the first time he'd ever backed away from her in any way—ever. "I know how to take care of myself."

"I know. I know." He sat down on the sofa, a good five feet away from her. "I have baby nerves. Fiona says they'll pass. And I hope they do soon. I think I'm about to wear everyone out, including Sam. And that's not easy, let me tell you."

"Easygoing Sam?" Jackie wanted her husband in her arms right now, but it was clear that wasn't happening. So she tried to follow Pete's lead and adopt nonchalance. "Tell me ranch gossip if you're not going to let me do wifelike things to you in the shower."

Pete gulped. She smiled at him, the picture of innocence. "Wifelike things?"

She nodded. "Things that perhaps involve kissing, soap, warm water and a very skilled pair of hands. Those kind of wifelike things."

He looked at her. "I see."

"So, you were saying about the ranch?" Jackie checked Pete's jeans, noting with pleasure that he wasn't as immune to her as he'd been acting. "Easygoing Sam doesn't appreciate you being moody?"

"I'm not moody," Pete said. "I've got a lot on my mind."

"Me, maybe?" Jackie said, unbuttoning her top.

He swallowed, watching her every move. "Maybe a little." His gaze lit on her lips, and then the expanse of skin beginning to show between the freed buttons.

He jumped to his feet. "You stay right there, Jackie. I'm going to shower. When I get out, I'll rub your feet."

He hurried off to the shower. Jackie closed her eyes, holding back a shriek of frustration. He was terrified of her doing anything that might hurt the babies.

She was going to scream if this kept up for three more months. "You're in for the surprise of your stubborn life, buddy," she said, getting up from the recliner and pulling off her clothes. She sneaked into the bathroom, where she could see Pete's strong, muscular body under the spray. His eyes were closed as he let the water beat down on his back—and an hour in the shower wasn't going to take care of the issue she could see that he had at the moment.

But she could. She slipped into the shower with him, moving her hands over his erection. Pete's eyes snapped open, and he started to pull away.

But now he was her prisoner. And she wasn't letting him go. She moved her hands along him, caressing him, until she felt his reluctance ebb away. He seemed to strengthen in her hands.

"I've missed you," she said. "You can't keep me in that recliner like a locked-away princess and not let me feel you."

His arms slowly went around her at last, and he held her against him, groaning a little as she stroked him. "I've missed you. You have no idea how much."

She pressed small kisses along his chin. "No more treating me like I'm going to break if you so much as touch me."

He leaned his chin against the top of her head, fully

under her spell. "I dream of touching you." Almost reluctantly, he took her breasts in his hands, cupping them, teasing the nipples. "You're scaring me. The doctor said—"

"I'm seducing you." She gently pushed his hands away. "Kiss me. You'll like it, I promise."

So he did. Jackie pushed up against him, her hands teasing him, torturing him, but then drawing him inexorably toward pleasure. It was such a relief to touch him, feel his strong body, that Jackie wanted more, and relief from the heat of remembering what Pete could do to her body.

"After the babies are born," Pete began, and Jackie said, "The honeymoon begins ASAP," and the next thing she knew, he was shuddering against her, holding her the way she'd wanted to be held, and letting her hold him.

His arms locked around her. "You did seduce me," Pete murmured against her wet hair, and Jackie smiled.

"Yes," she said, happy to have her stubborn cowboy back in her arms. "Never think about staying away from me again."

"You win," Pete said, "I'm only a man. Not a prince."

Jackie smiled. He was her prince, but she couldn't allow him to be a tyrant in matters of marital pleasure. He was just going to have to let her please him often.

AFTER JACKIE's rather skilled seduction of him—and Pete had to admit he'd loved every second—he made sure he put her right back in her recliner. "The home nurse says you are to stay still," he said, kissing her forehead to take the sting out of his words. "Not that I don't seriously appreciate your foxy side. But I have to think for the five of us. That means you have everything you need right here." He pointed to the TV remote, the portable phone, a glass of water and Fanny, whom he'd placed in her lap. "And I don't want you alone, either, Jackie, not even for fifteen minutes. Either me, or the home nurse, or Darla, or Fiona or even Jonas, if necessary, since he's still a doctor, must be with you."

"That's what the phone is for, Pete," Jackie said through gritted teeth. "So that people don't have to spend their days sitting here watching me like a nesting duck. I'm a nurse," she reminded him, as though Pete could ever forget it.

"But you're not a doctor," he said, dropping a kiss on her nose. "And these are my babies. I don't want to take any chances. So from now on, you don't move. I'll take care of everything."

She glared at him. "Pete, you're going to be a wonderful father. And I appreciate this newly protective side of you. Believe me when I say that in five years, I never thought you cared so much—"

"Well, you were wrong." He folded his arms across his chest. "I cared."

"But now you care a lot," she said. "Too much."

He shook his head. "Either the sofa, the bed or the recliner. But you, my love, will stay in a horizontal position until our little girls are ready to see their father's handsome face." He kissed her on the lips, ducking back when she took a gentle swipe at him. "Oh, my little hellcat. I do love you." He gently patted her tummy, then went into the kitchen. "So what can I make you for dinner, my turtledove?"

Pete smirked to himself. He was pretty certain that if he'd been anywhere near Jackie, that last statement would have gotten the remote launched at his head. His lady was impatient and on edge, and he couldn't blame her. Pete couldn't imagine being confined to a recliner.

"You probably think this is all my fault," he called out to her.

"Probably," she said, and he grinned.

"Egg salad?" he asked. "Or pancakes. Fiona sent the egg salad. I can whip up mean pancakes. Your choice, my love."

"I'm not hungry."

She'd been plenty hungry for him not thirty minutes ago. Pete frowned and walked back out to the den. "I know this is hard on you. I'm trying to help."

Jackie shook her head. "I'm sorry. I know you are. And it's not bad. I have all these wonderful books to read. There are three hundred channels on the TV. I'm catching up on movie classics, and that's really fun. I've been ordering DVDs on my laptop and building a collection of family movies between researching other wedding shops across the country. But it's not the same."

"Try being the guy who can't give his wife any pleasure at the moment," he said. "It's embarrassing."

"Embarrassing?" She looked surprised.

"What do you think? While I appreciate your efforts, it's not as much fun without you screaming hallelujahs in my ear, Jackie. It's bad for my ego." He thought about it for a minute, trying to explain. "It's like yelling into a canyon and nothing comes back."

"Coming without me isn't good?"

"It's not bad," he said, "but it's not as good, either."

"Oh," Jackie said. "I thought men just—"

He held up a hand. "Common misconception. But men are not cave-dwellers in search of the one-sided orgasm. Trust me. Some of us have evolved. And we like being joined in the hallelujah chorus. In fact, several hallelujah choruses. A hat trick is best."

Jackie nodded. "Thank you for explaining that. Now I'm even more hot and bothered."

"I knew it," he said. "It's best we leave sex off the menu for now. Back to the pancakes or whatever else your heart desires."

"My heart desires you."

He sighed. "You, my sweet, must just lie there and look pretty."

She threw a pillow that caught him square in the face. "What?"

"Go," Jackie said, sounding like she meant it. "And next time you think of me, think of me in my nurse's uniform, taking your temperature in a place you won't appreciate, you male chauvinist—"

"Hang on," Pete said, "I'm just saying—"

"I have knitting needles," she said. "You should go now." She brandished a needle from which hung a pink bootie that didn't look all that successful to him—not that he planned on mentioning it to his angel cake while she was in this rather surly mood.

"All right. I'm going to get pasta. With veggies, because that will be healthy. And when I get back, we'll have a picnic right here." He gave her his best how's-that-deal? smile and got a finger pointed at the door for his effort.

"I won't be gone long," Pete said. "I've got my cell phone if you need me, if you need anything at all—"

"Go!"

PETE RAN INTO Creed at the Italian family restaurant. "Why are you here?" he asked as he slid into the booth where his brother sat nursing a brewski.

"Fiona didn't cook anything tonight. She said we were on our own." Creed shrugged. "Usually she gets ruffled if some of us don't show up for dinner. But she's been acting a little moody lately."

"Must be something in the water." Pete thought about Jackie and decided she had cause to be as moody as she liked. "Is Aunt Fiona feeling all right?"

"She's fine." Creed shook his head, his black hair wild and unbrushed. He needed a shave, Pete noticed, or he was thinking about growing an unattractive mop on his face. And he looked glum. "Bode Jenkins came over, and the two of them had an unpleasant meeting of the minds, to choose polite terms."

Pete straightened. "What did Bode want?"

"I don't know. Burke told me about it. That's the only reason I can guess at what upset Fiona."

"That bastard," Pete said, "I'll kick his ass."

"No need. Judah already did. Sort of. As much as you can kick an old man's ass." Creed scratched his chin. "I think he just yelled at him and told him he'd kick him good if he didn't move his carcass off Callahan property. And Bode said it wasn't going to be Callahan property much longer, and then Fiona fainted. I think." Creed swallowed half his beer, then nodded. "Yeah. Jonas said she'd fainted."

"Damn," Pete said. "I can't tell whose butt I need to be laying out if you're going to change the facts every time you draw a breath."

"It happened so fast. Fiona's like a badger, you know, so we weren't too worried about her, but then Bode dropped his ace card and Fiona went lights out. Hell, Pete, I thought she'd kicked it."

Pete went cold. "She's tougher than that. She'll outlive us all."

"Yeah." Creed swallowed some more beer, then shook

his head. "Anyway, so now we all know about the secret Fiona's been hiding. She said we're losing the ranch."

Pete shook his head. "I guess."

Creed narrowed his eyes. "Did you already know?"

"I knew a little about it," Pete said, "though I was never sure Fiona had told me everything. You know how she dribbles out bits and pieces. And it's never clear exactly what's really going on."

"But you knew. And you didn't tell any of us." Creed looked mad as hell.

Pete shrugged. "She asked me not to."

"But you knew there wasn't going to be a ranch for any of us to win. You knew that all along. You would have let us head to the altar for no reason." Creed glared at him.

Pete shrugged. "You weren't in any danger, were you?"

"I might have been! And you would have let me walk the plank!"

"Nah."

"Oh, yes, you wouldn't have stopped me." Creed jutted his scraggly chin out. "Do you have any idea how much we've been worrying about this whole marriage bet?"

"Who's we?"

"The rest of us. Those of us who weren't picking out brides."

Pete shook his head. "As I recall, you were all too happy to let me be the fall guy."

"And so we were. But we didn't know Jackie would marry you at the time. Any of us might have ordered a bride. Gotten a subscription to an online dating service. I seriously thought about it." Creed gulped. "But marriage is not for the faint of heart, and my heart is faint when it comes to commitment."

"I know," Pete said sourly. "You weren't in any danger. So cool it."

"Still. Brothers shouldn't hold back pertinent information, especially when it comes to Fiona." Creed paused. "I've been sitting here thinking, and I've worked it over pretty well in my mind, and…I'm going back on the rodeo circuit."

Pete sighed. "Don't make a hasty decision."

"There's nothing else for us to do. We're all in the process of thinking through our options. Jonas put an offer on the ranch east of here. Judah's going back to rodeo for a while. Rafe is seriously considering hiring on with the Shamrock ranch. And Sam…well, he says he'll probably be Fiona's bodyguard. Or go do some bullfighting. He'd make a damn lousy clown, in my opinion. Wasn't very good at it before. Still, a man's got to do something, and if we have no livelihood here, then what the hell can any of us do? Can't sit around on our duffs watching our family home go up in a puff of smoke."

Pete shook his head. "Nothing good can come of Sam and bullfighting."

Creed shrugged. "He says someone has to hang around to make Bode's life a misery. He says he's either going to take his aggression out on Bode or on bulls. He hasn't decided yet."

"Marvelous," Pete said, "this is all just ducky as hell."

His cell phone rang. Pete pulled it from his pocket, snapping it open when he saw the call was from Darla.

"Pete?" Darla said. "Thank God I reached you. Your phone hasn't been ringing."

He frowned. Maybe the reception in the restaurant

was poor. "What's up?" he asked, his body tensing, his thoughts immediately on Jackie.

"It's nothing," Darla said, but she didn't sound like her normally bouncy self. Pete held the phone tightly against his ear so he could hear her. "At least I hope it's nothing. Jackie was having a little stomachache, a bit more cramping than usual, so she called me and I came over to sit with her. Then I decided to call the doctor and he suggested we swing her by the hospital."

Pete stood up, tossed some money on the table. He knew he shouldn't have let Jackie stand so long. Maybe hot showers weren't good for pregnant women. They'd had harsh words between them, perhaps a toxic stew for tiny angels. "I'll be right there."

He snapped the phone shut. "Jackie's gone to the hospital," he told Creed, his body feeling queer and not part of himself anymore as he hurried to his truck.

Dear God. Please let her be fine. I only just made her mine.

Chapter Seventeen

The scary—and amazing—part was that Pete was a father faster than he'd ever dreamed he could be. One day he was thinking *marriage,* and today Pete realized they hadn't bought cribs. Diapers. Toys. Hadn't even talked about it.

Pete wasn't even sure how they were going to fit three babies into the small guest room. But he looked at Jackie's worn-out face and thought she was beautiful, tough and strong, and he knew everything was going to be fine.

He smoothed her hair away from her face. He still didn't understand exactly what had gone wrong. Or maybe nothing had gone wrong. Perhaps the babies had just decided there was too little room inside his petite wife for all of them to be comfortable. He hadn't had a chance to talk to the doctor yet.

He kissed Jackie on the forehead. "Mrs. Callahan, you have three very small, very beautiful little daughters. And do you know something? They all have your cute nose."

Jackie smiled wanly. "They have all their fingers and toes?"

"They're perfect. Little angels."

His heart hammered inside him. What was he going

to do now? He had to learn how to bathe babies. He'd looked them over carefully as the nurses gently suctioned them, weighed them, measured them. It had taken every bit of self-control not to beg the nurses to be more careful with his tiny progeny—the babies looked so helpless, so fragile. More fragile than anything he'd ever seen in his life. Fanny was bigger and stronger than his daughters.

He was scared as hell.

"I love you," he said to Jackie.

"I love you, too." She closed her eyes.

"Jackie," he said, close to her ear so that she wouldn't feel like she had to open her eyes and look at him, "I'm... I'm losing it here."

She opened her eyes and reached for his hand to squeeze. "Everything is fine."

He swallowed. "You scared the hell out of me. I think I hurt you. Maybe we had too much...I mean, I can't bear that you were in pain."

She shook her head. "I've always wanted children. I didn't think I could have them. Whatever pain I had was such a small sacrifice that I've already forgotten about it."

He glanced around at the nurses, who were paying him no attention at all. Their whole focus was on his darling bundles of joy. But the emergency C-section weighed heavily on his mind. What if there'd been a problem? "Jackie," he whispered, "Is it okay with you if these are all the children we have? I don't think I can live with the fear of losing you."

But Jackie had fallen asleep so his agonized soul-searching was his alone. Pete took a deep breath and tried to get a grip on himself.

"Mr. Callahan," a nurse said, "we're going to take the babies down to neo-natal now."

The babies. He probably looked like a cold-hearted sonofagun not to be over there staring with pride at his sweet girls. But he was nervous. They'd been fixed up with tubes and warmers and things, and he didn't think he'd ever be able to change a diaper without worrying that he'd pull off a leg. Accidentally snap off a tiny toe. God, he'd seen corn kernels bigger than those toes. He gulped. "Thank you."

He looked back to Jackie, embarrassed that he didn't feel more for his daughters. Jackie was all he could think about. "Never again," he told her, though she slept like an enchanted princess. "No more pregnancies. This is it for me. I want the rest of our lives together to be one long Saturday night."

CREED FOUND PETE COLLAPSED face-down on Jackie's shoulder, even as Pete sat bunched in a chair beside her. Creed set the flowers and the huge pink-and-white teddy bears he'd brought on a table and sighed. "Pete. You're gonna have a helluva of a backache tomorrow."

Pete didn't move. In fact, he looked as dead to the world as Jackie. And in that moment Creed realized his brother loved Jackie Samuels with all his heart and soul. It hadn't been about the bet, though maybe that had provided a push. Pete was part of Jackie, and Jackie was part of Pete, and the two of them shared something that was missing in his own life.

Creed sighed and went to find his diminutive nieces. They were wailing in the nursery, shaking tiny fists while nurses tended to them. He had to admit that his nieces didn't look much like Callahans. They weren't brawny, or beefy or beautiful. "Whew, you'd think Pete might have turned out a little better gene material than that," he muttered.

But the nurses looked a lot more appealing. Creed perked up as three nurses hovered around the bassinets. There were tubes and breathing apparatuses and things that looked painful on his nieces, so Creed focused on the shapely nurses.

He didn't want a nurse, he decided. Jackie had been a nurse. Then she'd opened a bridal salon. And then she'd done this. He rubbed his chin, wondering where he'd ever find a woman that was the other half of him, as Pete had. The trouble with women was that you couldn't buy them and sell them like cattle or horses. If you got a bad one, you were stuck.

Stuck would be bad.

Pete could handle the situation they'd all gotten him into, because Pete was responsible. Creed liked to think of himself as more footloose. Actually, he was probably more in tune with his inner being and didn't need the security of another person. Pete was needy, Creed decided. This was all Jonas's fault. If Jonas hadn't left to go to a fancy Ivy League school up north, and then stayed the hell away to get his medical degree and training, Pete wouldn't have turned out to be Mr. Responsibility.

I'm not ready for any of what Pete's bitten off.

Fiona rushed to the nursery window. "Look at them! Oh, my! Have you ever seen anything more beautiful than those little babies?"

He had, but Fiona probably wouldn't take his observation well so he kept his mouth shut. "They're no bigger than newborn piglets," he observed, and Fiona popped him a smart one on the arm.

"They'll grow." She stared happily through the window, her whole body practically vibrating with joy.

Creed put his arm around his aunt, giving her a fond hug. "You've done yourself proud."

"I did?" She looked at him.

"Well, if you hadn't spurred Pete into marriage—"

He stopped when her face fell. "No, no. Focus on the babies. Look how cute they are! I think that one in the middle has your nose, Aunt Fiona."

Fiona looked distressed. "These children have no place to live. And it's all my fault."

Creed looked at her. "Why would it be your fault?"

"I lost the ranch." She gazed up at him with huge, tear-filled eyes. "And where are these babies going to grow up? Run? Play?"

"At Jackie's house?" Creed asked.

"Pooh. Jackie's house is no bigger than a dollhouse. I was there the other day. She doesn't even have a nursery set up."

He blinked. "Nothing?"

"Not even a crib. Besides which, there's probably only twelve hundred square feet in the entire cottage."

"I think that's Pete's business, Aunt Fiona," Creed said, his tone reluctant.

"These angels don't even have names! Callahan number 1, Callahan number 2 and Callahan number 3. What is that, I ask you?" Fiona peered through the glass. "Not that I care what anyone thinks, mind you, but for heaven's sakes, at least have names on the bassinets when my friends come to visit."

Creed shook his head. "That's for Pete and Jackie to decide."

"They're slow about it." Fiona looked disgusted, then brightened. "Creed, I think that little redheaded nurse is smiling at you," she said, giving him a playful dig in the side that the nurse noticed. She batted her eyes at Creed, and he stepped away from the window, his heart palpitating. In fact, he'd broken out in a nervous sweat.

His destiny was clear. He had to get out of Diablo. Fiona was done working on Pete, and if he wasn't careful, she'd turn her attention to *his* bachelor state. The sacrifice—Pete—had gone down like a newbie bull rider. And now there was no reason to worry about the ranch anymore.

She was going to work him like a bear in a circus. He did not want to be next on her to-do list.

"Don't you worry about a thing, Aunt Fiona," Creed said, giving her a kiss on the forehead even as he backed away from his plotting aunt and the attractive redhead eyeing him. "I'll see you later."

Fiona's gaze was on Pete's three daughters, and Creed made his getaway.

If he didn't watch out, he was going to end up like Pete—with a wife, babies and a gingerbread house. Creed broke into a run as he hit the exit.

"JACKIE," PETE SAID when she opened her eyes an hour later, "Look what the teddy-bear fairy brought."

He pointed to the three enormous bears sitting up on the table. "Our daughters won't be as big as those bears when they're in fifth grade."

Jackie smiled. "They'll grow. I just need to feed them."

He jumped to his feet, realizing his beautiful wife had to be hungry. "Can I get you something? A drink? Something to eat?"

"A new body." Jackie shifted with a groan. "Pete, what do you think about the babies?"

Pete straightened. "Um, they look just like their

mother. Gorgeous. They seem bossy, too. Very opinionated about what they want." He shot her a careful glance. "I like that in a woman, as you know."

Jackie looked at her husband. "Did you get within three feet of them?"

"Ah...not yet," he hedged. "But I will. When they aren't like tiny loaves of bread."

"Pete Callahan, I never thought I'd see the day when you were afraid of anything." Jackie smiled at him. "Although I don't think you were too happy when you locked yourself in the basement."

"I didn't—oh, hell." He sat down next to her. "Can you drink a beer? Wine? I feel like I need a small shot of courage."

Jackie was already tired again. "Go down and see our daughters. Then go celebrate."

"I'm not leaving you." Pete picked up her hand, caressing it with his lips. "I shouldn't have left you today."

"The babies were ready to be born, Pete. Whether or not you were there to stop it, they were coming."

He shook his head, and she knew her stubborn cowboy was having trouble dealing with everything. She loved him for it. "Don't worry. You're going to be a great father."

"How do you know? I haven't had any experience. I have no role model. I'd like to bottle them until they're eighteen, and then send them off to college."

"Pete." Jackie laughed. "You remind me of Mr. Dearborn."

"I'm nothing like Mr. Dearborn. I'm far better looking."

"Tell that to Jane. She will not agree." Jackie ran her fingers through Pete's shaggy black hair. She didn't think he'd touched a brush in twenty-four hours. Life had certainly changed a lot for her cowboy. "Do you want to go shave and change your clothes?"

"I'm not leaving. So back to Mr. Dearborn and why he gets to share my wife's mind when she thinks of me."

"He was a pain," Jackie said with a smile. "My most needy patient, by far. He wanted more attention, so he got it. And I knew he was trying to get my attention, but I couldn't help myself. He was cute when he complained. He did it so nicely, and I knew he was doing it on purpose."

Pete frowned. "But I'm not a complainer, nor am I needy."

Jackie laughed. "You're needy."

"My wife just had triplet daughters. I'm entitled to be a little off my normally rugged and independent game."

He pressed a kiss to her wrist, then put her hand down. "I have fantasies about getting in this hospital bed with you, Mrs. Callahan."

She patted the bed. "Bring it on, cowboy."

"You, me and at least a bed will be happening as soon as the doctor pronounces you healed. Until then, you're on a Pete diet." He slightly pulled away from her, leaning back in the uncomfortable chair. "So, don't you think we should discuss names?"

Jackie blinked. "Fiona, Molly and Elizabeth. Didn't you tell the nurses?"

He looked at her. "Did I miss a bulletin, wife?"

"Did we need to discuss it? I wouldn't think baby names are your thing, Pete."

"I think we should discuss everything."

"Then you choose some names."

Pete hesitated. "I haven't had time to think about names."

"Surely there are some that you like." Jackie waited, amused that her husband seemed to get more flustered by the moment.

"I don't know any girl names. And you've caught me off guard. I don't think well when I'm rattled." Pete gazed around the room as if looking for clues. "I was just thinking it was time to buy a baby book."

"I think we're past the book stage, husband. I'd go buy cribs and diapers, wash cloths, towels, that sort of thing," Jackie suggested.

Pete looked horrified. "We haven't bought anything. Jackie, we have to have car seats to get the babies home from the hospital." Pete stood up so fast he nearly knocked over the chair. "I've got a lot to do."

Jackie was about to say so *go do it* when the man who walked into her room made the words go completely away.

Chapter Eighteen

Pete bristled, stepping in front of Bode Jenkins and his caregiver. "Hello, Sabrina," Pete said politely. To the man standing next to her, carrying an umbrella he used as a walking stick, Pete said, "To what do we owe the honor of this unexpected visit, Jenkins?"

Bode grinned at him. Pete told himself no new father took a swing at visitors. He held his fire.

"Your folks mentioned you'd had your babies, Jackie," Bode said, ignoring Pete. "I come bearing gifts." He handed her some flowers, beautiful pink tulips in a vase, which she had set on the nightstand.

Pete glanced at Sabrina. She shrugged at him, clearly not aware of why Bode had had her drive him to see Jackie. Every protective instinct Pete possessed roared to life. "You've given your gift, now shove off, Jenkins."

"Have a seat, Sabrina," Bode told his caregiver after Sabrina had hugged Jackie, then he sat down himself. "Pete, I'm here to make you an offer you can't refuse."

"Try me."

Bode laughed. "Don't be so hasty, son. You've got three daughters to think about. They're tiny now, but one day they'll need a place to bring their friends. And later, their dates." He smiled at Jackie. "You'd be surprised how time flies."

"It's not flying now because you're still here." Pete frowned. "What the hell do you want, Jenkins?"

Bode stretched out his legs, glancing at Sabrina as if they shared a secret. "I'm proposing to sell you five acres of your ranch, Callahan. You can build a house there that'll fit this brood you've acquired." He smiled at Jackie. "A man needs room to spread out, darlin'."

Jackie started to say something, but Pete forestalled his gentle bride's words. "*Five* acres?" It was an insult, a slap in his face to embarrass him in front of Jackie and remind him that Bode had him by the shorts. "I don't require much room, Bode. Our family will do just fine where we are."

Bode raised a brow. "Three daughters, a wife and a big man all sharing a tiny house that used to be a rental property for an elderly woman who had no means? Come on, Pete. You could use five acres. You can at least have a garden patch on five acres."

Pete's blood was on full boil. "Whatever you did to my aunt makes business between you and me impossible."

"Oh, now. Don't be sore about that. Especially when I'm offering to let you have five acres, Callahan. You've got a family to think about. It's land you could at least sell if you needed money."

So I'm supposed to beg for the crumbs of my family home. Pete squared his jaw, forcing himself not to cold-cock another man on his daughters' birthday. It would be a bad thing to do. "And if I wanted to do business with you—which would be a cold day in Hell—what would it cost me?"

"Not a dime," Bode said.

Jackie's gaze was on Pete. Her eyes were huge with some emotion he couldn't name. If Bode had meant to shame him, he was doing an excellent job. The way the man put it, Pete couldn't provide for his own family—which, though none of Bode's business, was galling if people were to think that about a man who considered himself Mr. Responsibility. "Out," he told Bode, "get out. If you have business to discuss with me, don't do it here when my wife's just given birth, you miserable sack of—" He held himself back with great effort that choked the words in his throat. "Get out before I do something to you only my brothers would do better."

"Let him say his piece, Pete," Jackie said quickly. "We agreed all decisions would be made between us."

"No, we didn't," Pete replied. "You named the babies without me."

Jackie blinked. It seemed that she shrank back a little. Her hands clutched the sheets as she stared at him. *Oh, hell. Bode wants us to doubt our marriage, wants to find our weak link.* "Out," he told the man, "before I kick your ass up between your ears and roll you down the hall."

Sabrina got to her feet and helped Bode from his chair. The tall, white-haired man allowed her to do it, but he grinned at Pete. "Let me know, son, when you want to talk business. All I want is information about the silver mine hidden on my new property, and for your trouble, five acres is all yours."

Pete jammed his hands in his jeans so he wouldn't swing. He was going to be the bigger man here. And he and Jackie were not going to have their first argument just because of a jackass.

Bode and Sabrina left, after Sabrina hugged Jackie, surreptitiously whispering something in Jackie's ear.

"What?" Pete asked after they'd left. The urge to

move quickly, repair whatever damage Jenkins had done between him and Jackie, took him to his wife's side. "Why are you looking at me like that?"

"I'm not looking at you like anything," Jackie said. But her gaze fell to her hands.

"Jackie?" He felt her slipping away from him.

"I'm so tired right now," she murmured. "Good night, Pete."

She closed her eyes and he was left out, his hands in fists at his sides, even as he knew Bode Jenkins, that snake in the grass, had made a first strike.

JACKIE KNEW EXACTLY when Pete left. She feigned sleep, needing to gather her thoughts. What Bode had said about Pete needing more room scared her to death. It was true. There was no way she could insist that a big man share a bathroom and a tiny cottage with her and their daughters. It didn't make sense, and she'd been unreasonable.

Her house had been the last piece of herself she could keep, and she'd protected her turf without any thought of Pete's needs. She'd been so shocked by the pregnancy, and then finding out they were having multiple babies, that she hadn't considered living space until it was too late. She hadn't even decorated a nursery. She'd been too busy thinking about her new business.

Defense, she'd been playing defense.

A nurse came in to record her vitals. "How are you doing?"

"Fine. How are my daughters?" Jackie sat up, eager to hear.

"Doing fine and keeping everyone busy."

"When do I get to feed them?"

"In a little while, after you've rested."

Jackie looked at her. "Is my...husband at the nursery?"

The nurse shook her head. "No. His aunt and uncle are, though. They had an awful squabble a few moments ago with a visitor." She smiled at Jackie. "Your aunt won."

Bode had paid a visit to the nursery. She'd have to ask Sabrina what had happened later. Sabrina was on her side. She had whispered in her ear that Bode didn't mean any harm; he really just wanted to see the babies. And he was upset that he hadn't been invited to the wedding. But no one had been. There really hadn't been a wedding, not that she cared what Bode Jenkins thought. She wouldn't invite him, anyway, if he was always going to torture poor Fiona. "What happened?"

"I don't know exactly. She called him a thief, and he called her a mismanaging airhead. I thought she was going to lay him out. Her driver had to separate them." The nurse laughed. "We don't get many little elderly people raising a ruckus around here."

"Can you ask Fiona to come in here, please?" It was imperative that she speak to her.

"You don't need more visitors," the nurse said. "You need to rest."

Suddenly, Jackie knew exactly how Mr. Dearborn had felt—trapped and helpless. The exact way Pete was probably feeling right now, if she wasn't quick about putting things right.

But she'd learned a trick or two from Mr. Dearborn. "I was once a nurse here," she said, a little wistfully. "Sometimes I miss working with patients. And you're new at the hospital, aren't you?"

"I've been here three weeks." The nurse picked up her chart. "Is there anything I can get you?"

"Yes. You can get me Aunt Fiona," Jackie said, her voice sweetly determined. "I'll rest so much better once I see her cheery face."

The nurse walked to the door, smiling. "I heard you used to sneak some of your favorite patients chocolate. Particularly the difficult ones."

"Are you planning on bringing me some chocolate?" Jackie asked.

"Nope. But I'll get your aunt."

She left, and Jackie winced at the stitches in her stomach. "Good. I was about to get cranky with you," she muttered.

But then Fiona fluttered into the room, and Jackie launched her plan.

"The babies," Fiona said, "they are such darlings! I can't wait to hold them! How are you doing, my dear?"

She carefully leaned in to hug Jackie.

"I'm fine, Fiona," Jackie said, "but I'm afraid I need a huge favor."

"Babysitting, cooking, some new nighties from the store in town I hear you like shopping at?" Fiona said, eyeing her hospital gown.

"Darla's gone to get me some things. I didn't think I'd need a bag when she brought me to the hospital. We thought we would only be here for a quick check to soothe her nerves. I hadn't even packed a suitcase for the hospital. But I have something else that must be done. And you will have to keep it totally secret, please, Fiona. Absolutely under your hat."

"Oh, good," Fiona said, her face beaming. "Now what do you need me to do?"

"I NEED HELP," PETE TOLD JONAS. His brother sat at the rugged plank table in the bunkhouse, and the others—except Creed, who'd gone off somewhere, clearly out of cell phone reach because no one could get him to answer—lounged around the room, celebrating the birth of Pete's daughters and the successful hatching of The Plan.

But it wasn't a success yet, because his angels needed him. And their father planned to ride to their rescue.

After that, he'd rescue his wife from his total wipeout as a husband. Bode Jenkins wasn't going to win this round. "I need help from all of you."

"If this is about my nieces, I'll do anything except change diapers," Sam said. "And clean spit-up. Hurl is hard for me to look at."

"You're a moron," Judah said. "Babies don't hurl. Not much, anyway. Not like you do after a bender, for example."

Rafe lifted a beer in Sam's direction. "You'll have to toughen up, Sam. Pete's not going to be sleeping much for the next couple of weeks, and we all need to help him out. When do the babies leave the hospital, Pete?"

"I'm not sure. They only weighed about four pounds each." That alone scared the hell out of Pete. "Does anybody remember what we weighed?"

"It would say on your birth record," Jonas said, "and Fiona's probably got that buried somewhere."

"It doesn't matter. I'm pretty sure I wasn't four pounds." He remembered Sam when he'd arrived at the ranch. Sam had been about as big as a ten-pound sack of new potatoes. Pete's daughters were more like good-sized Idaho spuds. He glanced around at his brothers, not liking the new helpless feelings swamping him. "They're so small they could be in the hospital for a month."

"No," Jonas said. "We have to think positive. The delivering physician said that they were healthy, just underweight. That's a good sign."

Pete drew a relieved breath. "Jackie and I made no plans for anything."

"We know." Rafe grinned. "You've been very disorganized about becoming a father, which isn't like you at all. But we've been impressed that you've pulled it off, Pete. We didn't give you a snowball's chance, frankly."

"Glad you've got my back." The jackasses were ribbing him, and he appreciated the brotherly love but he still felt as if a whirlwind had blown into his life, spewing everything in forty directions. "So, are you going to help me or not?"

"What do you need?" Judah asked.

"No diapers," Sam reminded him.

"I need a nursery," Pete said. "I'd make you a list, but I have no idea what babies need."

"You want us to round up all your baby stuff?" Jonas said.

"Right." Pete nodded. "Diapers, cribs, the works."

Sam looked scared. "You want us to make a nursery?"

"It's a lot to ask. But you can do it." Pete sat straight, still boiling mad about Bode's visit. "It's got to work. My turtledove doesn't want to leave her house. Bode's offered me five acres of Rancho Diablo land in exchange for me telling him where the silver mine is."

They all stared at him.

"Silver mine?" Judah repeated. "Is that rumor making the rounds again?"

"Yes." Pete nodded. "But never mind that. It was the look on Jackie's face that warned me I have to take drastic steps. She was actually *listening* to the old coot."

"There's no silver mine," Jonas said. "So who cares what he thinks?"

"There's no nursery, either. Bode told Jackie I wouldn't be happy in her house. That it was too small. That a man needed to spread out. And she looked crushed." He took a deep breath, still angry. "Bode must be the one who locked me in the basement. And searched the house. That's why Fiona's jars and everything she'd stored were destroyed in the basement. I know he did it."

"Because he was looking for silver?" Judah asked.

"Exactly." Pete nodded. "That's why he wants the ranch."

"There's no silver," Sam said, "there's nothing but hard work here. And the Diablos."

They sat silently. Ghostly horses that ran free across the ranch, full of spirit that never could be tamed, their midnight-black manes and tails flying. They were the treasure of Rancho Diablo.

"I saw Fiona's friend the other day," Sam murmured.

Everyone stared at Sam.

"And?" Pete prompted.

"He was on a black-and-white horse, looking down the mesa at our house." Sam shrugged. "He raised a hand when he saw me, and then he left."

Pete shook his head. "Maybe Fiona gives him blackberry jelly or canned asparagus from the basement. Have any of us considered just asking her why Running Bear visits her every year?"

They all shook their heads at him. Pete sighed to himself. It didn't matter. He was moving on, if Jackie would have him forever. She just had to want him as much as he wanted her. Otherwise he'd be like one of the lobos, howling every night at her door. "What are we going to do about Fiona? And Burke?" he asked suddenly.

"I haven't entirely surrendered to the notion that Bode's getting our land," Jonas said. "In the meantime, I did make an offer on the ranch east of here. We can set up operations there. Fiona and Burke can manage the new place, if it comes to that."

Pete felt slightly better that there was a plan for their extended family members. "I haven't surrendered, either," he said, feeling a growl start in his body. "Even if Bode does get the ranch, he's not going to sabotage my marriage." Things were dicey enough. He did know one thing: It would be a cold day in Hell before he gave up one small part of his marriage to anyone, or anything.

"First things first," Rafe said. "We've got baby rig to shop for, and that alone is a tall order. Do you know if Jackie has a particular color she wants for the nursery? I think color scheme may be important to a woman."

Pete thought about Jackie's white, lacy bedroom, a place he couldn't wait to be again, with her, holding her, making her his. "White. Completely white. Maybe some pink, but white and lacy and all little girl."

"Not that I know what I'm talking about," Judah said, "but isn't white supposed to pick up dirt easily? Is it a wise choice for three little infants who are going to do tons of…things Sam doesn't want to clean up?"

Pete smiled at his brothers, happier than he'd ever been in his life. "All white," he said, "and very, very soft. Like rose petals."

"Jeez, you've got it bad," Sam said.

"I hope I never say anything that unfortunate," Judah agreed. "Are you aware that you are starting to sound like Creed with his poetic soul? And I wouldn't be bragging about it, either."

Pete grinned. "One day," he said, "you'll find

yourselves wearing wedding rings, and you won't be crying. And I'll get to enjoy every moment of your transformation."

"Great." Jonas stood. "Let's head out. We've got a lot of work to do."

Chapter Nineteen

In the end, Fiona got wind of the nursery scheme, and that meant the Books 'n' Bingo Society got involved, which pretty much meant the entire town pitched in on the project. There were people coming and going for days. There was sawing, hammering, painting and elderly people taking Fanny for walks so she wouldn't go crazy from all the noise in the small house. Pete was only dimly aware of what was going on. He spent almost every second at the hospital with Jackie and the babies, only leaving to shower at Rancho Diablo. He had a toothbrush and a few changes of clothes at Jackie's but he hadn't moved totally in yet. They'd only been married for a few months, and he'd been traveling back and forth between her place and his, making sure she stayed in her recliner, and working at the ranch.

So when he finally took Jackie and the babies home, even he was shocked at what had happened to her house. The guest bedroom had been gutted. Two closets had been cut out and shelved, and at least twenty baby dresses hung in them. He couldn't tell how many nighties and other clothes were stacked neatly on the shelves, but there were even tiny baby socks and shoes. Pete thought it looked like an entire department store had been bought out. The hardwood floors gleamed. The walls were repainted a soft white, and a pink-roses-and-lace curtain topper hung over the window. Three white cribs lined a wall, each with pink-and-white gingham sheets and comforters, and even mobiles from which miniature giraffes, monkeys, and elephants hung. Their names—Fiona, Molly and Elizabeth—were painted on plaques above each bed. On a white table nearby, diapers, wipes, fluffy towels and washcloths were neatly stacked. There was a rocking chair, a swing, a huge pink stroller and bouncy seats.

They wouldn't have to buy anything for years.

He turned to see the joy he knew would be on Jackie's face. She looked stunned—and not too happy.

"What did you do?" she asked him, her brown eyes huge.

"I didn't do anything. I just asked for a little help from my brothers. And everybody else pitched in. We'll be writing thank you notes for months." He couldn't believe how perfect the nursery was. It was everything little babies would dream of, if they dreamed of anything except being held and fed. "Do you like it?"

Jackie sank into the rocker, still staring at the room. She glanced at the babies in the car carriers they'd brought in. Fiona, Molly and Elizabeth were sound asleep, nestling under pink blankets and without a care in the world. "I don't know what to say," Jackie said. "It's beautiful. I've never seen anything like it."

"Good." Pete grinned at her, totally pleased with himself. "This is a comfortable room even for a man. I'm going to be in that rocker more than you are. It glides back and forth, and the baby monitor is right here. I'll be able to call you whenever I want something."

He was so proud. He was trying so hard. Jackie

wanted to cry. Having to burst his happiness was going to be the hardest thing she'd ever done.

"Pete," she said, reaching out to take her husband's hand, "maybe I should have talked to you first."

"About what?"

He looked at her and Jackie sighed. "I was going to sell the house."

His handsome face stayed completely immobile. A tiny tickle of worry ran through Jackie. "I have to," she said. "You would never be happy here. You hadn't even brought most of your stuff here. It's a doll's house suitable for a single woman. But not for a man, and not for a family."

Pete's face darkened. "You shouldn't listen to Bode. He doesn't know me."

"I know." Jackie squeezed his hand. "You're the one who said that one bathroom wasn't enough for three teenage girls."

"This is true," Pete said gruffly. "A nightmare in the making. I advise against it. But we could have made the girls observe a lottery system."

She looked around the room. "This is a beautiful nursery, Pete. Thank you so much." She took a deep breath. "I'm so sorry. I should have talked to you about it. I spoke to your Aunt Fiona, but I guess she figured we had some things to work out between us before she helped me list the house. It's not that Bode was right about everything, but he did make me realize that I hadn't been thinking about my husband enough."

"It's your house. You can do whatever you want with it." But his voice was flat, dull.

She glanced around the room, her gaze taking in the nursery. "I love you, Pete Callahan."

"Where are you thinking of moving?" Pete asked her, and Jackie looked at him.

"Wherever you are," she said softly.

"Oh," he said, "why didn't you say that in the beginning?"

He was hurt, and she wouldn't have hurt him for the world. "I want to start our marriage with a clean slate. I want a place that's ours. So," she said, standing on tiptoe to lightly brush a kiss against his lips, "Since I picked our daughters' names, don't you think you should have a say in our daughters' new home? Wherever that is?"

Pete grinned, realizing Saturday nights were turning into forever, after all. "I love you, Jackie Callahan," he said. "Don't ever scare me like that again. I thought you were giving up on us."

"No," Jackie said, "the only change I really wanted in my life was you."

"Change is good," Pete said, taking his wife in his arms. He glanced at his three daughters sleeping peacefully, and Fanny dozing on the fluffy pink rug, and then he kissed Jackie the way he planned on kissing her for the rest of her life, with every ounce of love he had in his heart for her.

And that was the one thing that wasn't ever going to change.

Epilogue

On the very last day in May—as soon as he could get her to the altar after the babies were born—Pete married Jackie at Rancho Diablo. He wouldn't have traded the speed wedding in Santa Fe for anything, but it was a treat to see how Fiona and her friends had outdone themselves today. Pete grinned as he watched about five hundred guests mill across the ranch where tents and awnings had been set up. They'd invited their friends out to show how much they appreciated everything that had been done for Jackie and Pete and the girls, and even Fanny. But mostly, for Pete, today was about honoring Jackie and showing her how much he loved her.

"Your parents would be so proud, nephew," Fiona said. "How I wish they could have been here."

"I love you, Aunt Fiona," Pete said, hugging his pink-dressed aunt. "None of this would ever have happened without you."

She smiled at him, and watched Jackie mingle with the guests. "Probably not." She giggled. "But you were ever willing to take direction."

"I thought you always said I was a hellion."

"Indeed." Fiona smiled. "And I wouldn't have had you any other way. Now find your bride. I have babies to hold. And should I mention to Creed it's high time to think about a bride of his own? I was just telling Burke that if anybody needs the rough edges knocked off by a woman, it's Creed."

Fiona went off, and Pete minded his aunt by taking his beautiful wife in his arms. "It's time," he told her.

"For what?" Jackie asked

"The honeymoon night."

She looked at him. "Honeymoon night?"

"Tonight," he said, giving her a husbandly kiss, "we're getting away for a couple of hours to a hidden place, just the two of us. We have a date for a romantic dinner set up by the Books 'n' Bingo ladies."

She looked at him, her gaze wide. "That sounds wonderful!"

He gave her a fast kiss on the nose. "They don't call me Mr. Romance for nothing."

"That's something I didn't know," she teased.

He pulled her close. "Mr. Romance has another surprise for his new bride. In October, just as the weather will be getting a bit nippy here, I'll be seeing you in a bikini in Hawaii. That wedding gown is beautiful, but I can't wait to see you in something skimpier."

"Oh, Pete!" Jackie pressed up against him for a kiss he thought was distinctly approving of his plans, until she had one of those little mommy worries that afflicted her occasionally, and which he found incredibly sweet. "But who will watch the babies while we're honeymooning?" Jackie asked, looking adorably concerned.

Clearly his bride hadn't figured out he was also Mr. Responsible. "Look at my three daughters," Pete said, "do they look like they're going to suffer with Dr. Jonas, assorted uncles, Aunt Fiona, Burke and a brigade of townspeople to wrap around their minuscule fingers? I had people fighting over the babysitting calendar."

Jackie smiled as he kissed her in front of the entire gathering. "The best thing I ever did was marry you, cowboy."

"I know," he said, "now let's go get you out of that magic wedding gown. It's magically making me want you."

"I thought you didn't believe in magic," Jackie said.

He carried her toward his truck as their friends and family tossed rose petals on them and called out congratulations. "I do now," he said. "Every time I touch you, I believe."

"I love you, Pete," she said, and it was the most magical thing he'd ever heard, besides sweet baby noises and his little wife saying *I do, and I always did* at the rose-festooned altar. He was a happy, happy man.

And somewhere in the distance, Pete could hear hooves, running wild and free, over Rancho Diablo land.

Magic.

* * * * *

Creed is the next Callahan to find himself in danger of being dragged down the aisle.
Watch for the next book in Tina Leonard's
CALLAHAN COWBOYS *miniseries,*
THE COWBOY'S BONUS BABY.

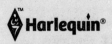

COMING NEXT MONTH

Available June 14, 2011

#1357 THE MAVERICK'S REWARD
American Romance's Men of the West
Roxann Delaney

#1358 FALLING FOR THE NANNY
Safe Harbor Medical
Jacqueline Diamond

#1359 A COWGIRL'S SECRET
The Buckhorn Ranch
Laura Marie Altom

#1360 THE DADDY CATCH
Fatherhood
Leigh Duncan

REQUEST YOUR FREE BOOKS!
2 FREE NOVELS PLUS 2 FREE GIFTS!

Harlequin®

American Romance®

LOVE, HOME & HAPPINESS

YES! Please send me 2 FREE Harlequin American Romance® novels and my 2 FREE gifts (gifts are worth about $10). After receiving them, if I don't wish to receive any more books, I can return the shipping statement marked "cancel." If I don't cancel, I will receive 4 brand-new novels every month and be billed just $4.24 per book in the U.S. or $4.99 per book in Canada. That's a saving of at least 15% off the cover price! It's quite a bargain! Shipping and handling is just 50¢ per book in the U.S. and 75¢ per book in Canada.* I understand that accepting the 2 free books and gifts places me under no obligation to buy anything. I can always return a shipment and cancel at any time. Even if I never buy another book, the two free books and gifts are mine to keep forever.

154/354 HDN FDKS

Name _____ (PLEASE PRINT)

Address _____ Apt. #

City _____ State/Prov. _____ Zip/Postal Code

Signature (if under 18, a parent or guardian must sign)

Mail to the **Reader Service:**
IN U.S.A.: P.O. Box 1867, Buffalo, NY 14240-1867
IN CANADA: P.O. Box 609, Fort Erie, Ontario L2A 5X3

Not valid for current subscribers to Harlequin American Romance books.

Want to try two free books from another line?
Call 1-800-873-8635 or visit www.ReaderService.com.

* Terms and prices subject to change without notice. Prices do not include applicable taxes. Sales tax applicable in N.Y. Canadian residents will be charged applicable taxes. Offer not valid in Quebec. This offer is limited to one order per household. All orders subject to credit approval. Credit or debit balances in a customer's account(s) may be offset by any other outstanding balance owed by or to the customer. Please allow 4 to 6 weeks for delivery. Offer available while quantities last.

Your Privacy—The Reader Service is committed to protecting your privacy. Our Privacy Policy is available online at www.ReaderService.com or upon request from the Reader Service.

We make a portion of our mailing list available to reputable third parties that offer products we believe may interest you. If you prefer that we not exchange your name with third parties, or if you wish to clarify or modify your communication preferences, please visit us at www.ReaderService.com/consumerschoice or write to us at Reader Service Preference Service, P.O. Box 9062, Buffalo, NY 14269. Include your complete name and address.

HAR11

Harlequin® Blaze™ brings you
New York Times *and* USA TODAY *bestselling author*
Vicki Lewis Thompson with three new steamy titles
from the bestselling miniseries SONS OF CHANCE

Chance isn't just the last name of these rugged
Wyoming cowboys—it's their motto, too!

Read on for a sneak peek at the first title,
SHOULD'VE BEEN A COWBOY

Available June 2011 only from Harlequin® Blaze™.

"THANKS FOR NOT TURNING ON THE LIGHTS," Tyler said. "I'm a mess."

"Not in my book." Even in low light, Alex had a good view of her yellow shirt plastered to her body. It was all he could do not to reach for her, mud and all. But the next move needed to be hers, not his.

She slicked her wet hair back and squeezed some water out of the ends as she glanced upward. "I like the sound of the rain on a tin roof."

"Me, too."

She met his gaze briefly and looked away. "Where's the sink?"

"At the far end, beyond the last stall."

Tyler's running shoes squished as she walked down the aisle between the rows of stalls. She glanced sideways at Alex. "So how much of a cowboy are you these days? Do you ride the range and stuff?"

"I ride." He liked being able to say that. "Why?"

"Just wondered. Last summer, you were still a city boy. You even told me you weren't the cowboy type, but you're…different now."

He wasn't sure if that was a good thing or a bad thing. Maybe she preferred city boys to cowboys. "How am I different?"

"Well, you dress differently, and your hair's a little longer. Your face seems a little more chiseled, but maybe that's because of your hair. Also, there's something else, something harder to define, an attitude…"

"Are you saying I have an attitude?"

"Not in a bad way. It's more like a quiet confidence."

He was flattered, but still he had to laugh. "I just admitted a while ago that I have all kinds of doubts about this event tomorrow. That doesn't seem like quiet confidence to me."

"This isn't about your job, it's about…your…" She took a deep breath. "It's about your sex appeal, okay? I have no business talking about it, because it will only make me want to do things I shouldn't do." She started toward the end of the barn. "Now, where's that sink? We need to get cleaned up and go back to the house. Dinner is probably ready, and I—"

He spun her around and pulled her into his arms, mud and all. "Let's do those things." Then he kissed her, knowing that she would kiss him back, knowing that this time he would take that kiss where he wanted it to go. And she would let him.

Follow Tyler and Alex's wild adventures in
SHOULD'VE BEEN A COWBOY
Available June 2011 only from Harlequin® Blaze™
wherever books are sold.

SPECIAL EDITION

Life, Love and Family

LOVE CAN BE FOUND IN THE MOST UNLIKELY PLACES, ESPECIALLY WHEN YOU'RE NOT LOOKING FOR IT...

Failed marriages, broken families and disappointment. Cecilia and Brandon have both been unlucky in love and life and are ripe for an intervention. Good thing Brandon's mother happens to stumble upon this matchmaking project. But will Brandon be able to open his eyes and get away from his busy career to see that all he needs is right there in front of him?

FIND OUT IN

WHAT THE SINGLE DAD WANTS...

BY *USA TODAY* BESTSELLING AUTHOR

MARIE FERRARELLA

AVAILABLE IN JUNE 2011
WHEREVER BOOKS ARE SOLD.

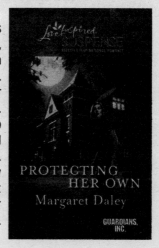

INTRIGUE